THE BOBBSEY TWINS ON BLUEBERRY ISLAND

"Come," the gypsy said. "I'll lead you to the very spot."

The Bobbsey Twins on Blueberry Island

By

LAURA LEE HOPE

GROSSET & DUNLAP
Publishers • New York

Cover illustration by Pepe Gonzalez.

Published in 2004 by Grosset & Dunlap, a division of Penguin Young Readers Group, 345 Hudson Street, New York, New York 10014.
GROSSET & DUNLAP is a trademark of Penguin Group (USA) Inc.
THE BOBBSEY TWINS® is a registered trademark of Simon & Schuster, Inc.

Printed in the U.S.A.

ISBN 0-448-43761-9

3 5 7 9 10 8 6 4 2

CONTENTS

CHAPTER I

MYSTERY MONEY

"THAT was a wonderful ride around the lake, Bert!" exclaimed Nan Bobbsey as the launch *Tall Timber* came toward the dock of the lumberyard which their father owned. "You're a good pilot."

"Glad you liked it." Bert grinned. He was Nan's twelve-year-old twin and, like her, had brown hair and eyes. He held a junior navigator's license.

Freddie, their younger, blond brother, put a hand on Bert's shoulder. "Bert can do everything!" the little boy declared proudly.

"Yes," Freddie's six-year-old twin, Flossie, chimed in as the breeze ruffled her blond curls. "Bert kept you from falling overboard! Remember?"

Nan looked across the water at the green, wooded islands which dotted Lake Metoka. "It would be fun to camp over there some time," she said.

Her twin winked. "I think we're going to," he said. "But I can't tell you any more about it right now."

The others begged for information, but Bert would give none. "Dad and I have a kind of secret. If a certain thing happens—well, you'll know it sometime."

"All right, meanie," said Flossie. "Anyhow, I'm glad Daddy bought this boat for the lumberyard. But I wish our family had one, too—just for us. Then when it's hot on land we could live on the boat out in the middle of the lake."

"Ho! Ho! Where would we all sleep?" Freddie asked her.

At this there came a chuckle from an older person on board. He was Sam Johnson, a man who drove a truck for Mr. Bobbsey's lumberyard. He and his wife Dinah lived on the third floor of the Bobbsey home. Dinah helped Mrs. Bobbsey with the housework.

"Guess you'd have to be stacked up like wheat cakes to sleep all your family on this boat," Sam remarked, still chuckling.

As the *Tall Timber* slid smoothly through the open doorway of the red boathouse, Bert said admiringly, "This new launch is super!"

"It sure is," said Freddie.

The *Tall Timber* was a thirty-foot, open

launch with a small cabin forward for the pilot and passengers. Everyone climbed out, and the twins thanked Sam for going with them. As he walked off, the children lingered on the dock alongside the boathouse to wait for a shaggy white dog that came bounding toward them. He held a large paper bag in his teeth.

"Here, Snap!" called Freddie joyfully. "What's in the bag? Bring it to me."

Instead of obeying, Snap circled the boy warily and was about to run off when Freddie caught him.

"Get the bag, Flossie," he cried, "while I hold him."

Flossie took the bag from Snap's jaws, then sat down on the dock to examine the contents.

"It's a game!" she exclaimed, drawing a box from the bag. "Daddy must have bought it and sent it by Snap as a joke."

Nan went to sit beside her sister. "It's a money game. See, there are paper coins and packages of toy five- and ten-dollar bills," she said.

"Ooh! I'm rich!" cried Flossie jokingly. "You add them up, Nan. My 'rithmetic isn't very good."

Nan took the box and began to count the bills while the others watched. At that moment Mr. Bobbsey, tall and good-looking, drove up and parked the family's station wagon near by.

"My goodness, where did you find all the

money?" he asked, smiling, as he joined the children.

"Dad, didn't you buy this game for us?" Bert asked. "Snap just brought it in this paper bag."

"No," his father said. "Some child must have lost the game and Snap found it."

"Oh!" Nan cried out suddenly. "There's a lot of real money in with these paper bills!" She held up a stack of ten-dollar bills bound with a purple band on which was stamped in large numerals: *$500.*

"Wow!" exclaimed Bert as the others crowded around. "Five hundred dollars in tens! Let's see it."

As he took the money, Nan said, "There's some handwriting on the band."

"Yes," Bert replied. "It says, 'Aunt Emma's Money.' I think I'll count it." He sat down beside Nan.

"This is amazing!" Mr. Bobbsey exclaimed. "Who would hide that amount of money in a child's game?"

"And where did Snap find it?" Freddie asked.

Flossie puckered her lips. "Who is Aunt Emma?" she said.

"It's sure mysterious," Bert remarked, looking up at his father. "Dad, there are only four hundred and ninety dollars here. I've counted it twice. Someone must have taken out a ten-dollar bill."

Snap had been watching with great interest. Now he drew nearer to Bert. Apparently feeling that he had first claim on the packet of greenbacks, he suddenly snatched it from Bert's hand and raced toward the street.

"Come back here, Snap!" screamed Flossie.

All the twins ran after their pet, but the mischievous dog pranced just out of their reach. Bert finally overtook him.

Snap, finding himself cornered, made a dash for the pier. As he scampered onto it, Nan cried, "Stop him! He'll jump off—"

Snap already had plunged into the water.

"Oh!" cried Freddie. "The money will get lost!"

Bert paused just long enough to remove his sneakers. Then he, too, dived into the lake.

"Bert's a good swimmer, but Snap can go fast too," Nan said as they watched the two.

"Snap! Come back here!" Mr. Bobbsey called loudly.

The dog turned in the water and started back. He managed to swim clear of Bert and then disappeared beneath the low-slung dock.

"Remember, Snap was once a circus dog," Mr. Bobbsey said. "You never can tell what tricks he may play."

"Oh! Here he comes from the other end of the dock!" cried Nan a few moments later.

Snap was running toward them from the shore end of the dock. He had clambered up the bank after swimming the length of the pier.

"The money's gone!" Freddie exclaimed, looking disappointed.

As Snap shook himself and showered them all with spray, Nan hurried toward Bert, who had seen Snap's return and was climbing up the ladder at the front end of the dock.

"The money must be in the water, Bert," she called to him. "Snap lost it."

Bert waved and went back down again to look for the packet of bills.

Freddie lay flat upon the dock and peered

through a large crack between the
think I see it," he called out after a m
"There's something green on a big post un
neath here."

Bert heard his brother and swam quickly under the pier.

"He's got it!" exclaimed Freddie.

In another minute Bert was climbing up the ladder again, holding the precious money triumphantly.

"Good for you!" said Mr. Bobbsey as he took the bills from his son. "I'll count these and see if all the money is here." Then, as he saw Snap eyeing him, "No! Over there, Snap!" He pointed to the station wagon. "No more tricks!"

Snap's tail drooped, and he walked reluctantly away to sit on the ground beside the family car.

Mr. Bobbsey counted the money. "It's all here and in good condition," he told the anxious children. "Now the next thing to do is drive Bert home for dry clothes, then we'll deliver this money to the police station."

The twins hurried to the car. Snap jumped into his usual place in the rear, and Mr. Bobbsey headed for home.

When they reached the house, Nan and her father went to tell Mrs. Bobbsey what had happened. Freddie and Flossie, meanwhile, hurried into the kitchen to tell Dinah.

The plump woman threw up her hands in amazement as she sank into a chair. "Well, of all things!" she exclaimed. "Don't tell me you all have found another mystery!"

The Bobbsey Twins were always finding little mysteries to solve, sometimes at home and at other times when they were on trips.

"Maybe we *are* going to have a mystery to find Aunt Emma," said Flossie. "And Snap is a hero dog to find her money, even if he was naughty."

Dinah called Snap in for his dinner. "That's a mighty important mouth you got there, Mr. Snap," she said, laughing. "I've got to respect a mouth that's been carrying around hundreds of dollars. Yes, sir! I'll just put a little of the steak that's left in with your dog food."

Flossie and Freddie laughed, and so did Dinah, as Snap gobbled up the extra good dinner in his bowl. Snoop, the Bobbseys' black cat, sat by and watched, as if to say, "That lucky dog!" Snoop had only cat food.

A few minutes later Bert came running downstairs in dry clothes, and the four children and their father set out. At the police station steps they met Chief Malone, who was just leaving.

"Why, hello, Mr. Bobbsey!" he said and greeted the twins. He smiled pleasantly and invited the callers inside.

Bert told him how Snap had found the bag containing the mysterious money. "And this is the packet which was in the game with the toy bills," he added, handing it to the chief.

The officer counted the bills. "I'll give you a receipt for this," he said. "We've had no report of this amount of money being lost by someone named Aunt Emma or anyone else. But we'll keep it safe here for ninety days. Then, if it isn't claimed, the money will be given back to the finder."

"Oh, my!" exclaimed Flossie. "What would Snap do with all that money?"

"Buy dog bones, I guess," said Freddie.

The chief laughed. "I reckon he'll be glad to turn it over to the Bobbsey twins," he said.

Bert grinned. "I wouldn't mind that at all," he said. "There's a dandy movie camera I've been admiring."

"But what about poor Aunt Emma?" Nan asked. "We want her to get her money back."

"Of course," replied Bert. "I was only joking."

"No doubt we'll hear from her," the officer assured the Bobbseys as he made out a receipt for the four hundred and ninety dollars.

The Bobbseys were about to leave the police station, when a woman hurried in. She looked white and worried.

"I've been robbed! All my money was stolen!" she exclaimed to the officer at the desk.

The Bobbseys looked at one another. Was this Aunt Emma?

CHAPTER II

A FUNNY MIX-UP

THE BOBBSEY twins waited eagerly to hear what else the woman who had been robbed would say.

"Please tell your whole story," the police officer requested. "But first, what is your name?"

"Mrs. Sara Brown."

So this was not Aunt Emma! The twins were disappointed but listened attentively as Mrs. Brown told the rest of her story.

"Someone snatched my purse just as I was getting into the bus to go home."

"That's the tenth report we've had of purse stealing in the past few days," the chief said.

"Then I'm glad we brought all that money to you," Freddie remarked. "Somebody might have stolen it from us."

"That's right," Chief Malone agreed.

As the twins and their father left police headquarters and started home, Bert said, "I think we'd better run an ad in the *Lakeport News* to tell 'Aunt Emma' that we found her money."

"Oh, yes," Nan agreed quickly. "We'll write it tonight."

"You must get it to the newspaper office in the morning if you want it in Sunday's paper," Mr. Bobbsey said. "And I think it's a good idea."

That evening after dinner Bert went to the living-room desk to compose the advertisement for the *Lakeport News*.

Nan watched her twin scribbling on several sheets of paper, then remarked, "You'd better not make it too long, Bert. The ad rates are high, and that much will cost a fortune."

Bert looked mysterious. "Oh, I was doing something else on those pages. I've already written the ad."

Nan looked at her brother curiously. What was Bert's secret, she wondered. Maybe she would find out soon!

Just then the twins' pretty mother came into the room, and Bert said, "How does this ad sound?

" 'Found. Aunt Emma's money. Claimant must show proof of ownership. Write the Bobbsey Twins, Lakeport.' "

"You must tell the date on which it was found," said Bert's mother. "Otherwise, the ad is fine."

Bert ran upstairs to his room to get the new typewriter which he had received for Christmas, and brought it downstairs. He and Freddie roomed together, so Bert used the desk in the living room when he had evening homework to do.

After he had typed the ad Bert still seemed to be busy doing something with pencil and paper.

"What are you working on?" Nan asked him.

Bert glanced up and saw his father looking at him. He gave him a slight wink, and they both smiled.

"Oh!" Nan exclaimed. "Has it something to do with that secret you and Daddy have?"

"It has a lot to do with it, or at least, I hope it has," her twin replied. "You'll know about it pretty soon, one way or another."

Nan laughed. "I think I'll go to bed before I start asking questions."

She bade them all good night and went up to the room she shared with Flossie, who was already asleep. Seven dolls of all sizes had been placed in the little girl's bed while she was huddled at the foot to give them room. Laughing to herself, Nan took out the dolls and tucked Flossie back under the bedclothes.

The next morning Bert hurried to the breakfast table after the rest of the family were seated.

"Sorry, Mother," he apologized. "I overslept."

Mrs. Bobbsey smiled at him. "You stayed up pretty late, I'm afraid, working on your—" She stopped as Bert made a quick gesture. Then she said, "Try to do your work in daylight, dear. It isn't so hard on your eyes, and you can get to bed earlier."

"Okay, Mother," Bert answered. He finished his breakfast quickly, then excused himself to telephone the police station.

In a few moments he was back. "They've had no report about Aunt Emma's money," he announced, "so we'd better go to the newspaper office and put the ad in the paper."

"Are you twins going to ride your bicycles?" Mr. Bobbsey asked, "or shall I drop you off on my way to the office?"

"A ride would be fine, Dad," Bert said. "I want to stop at Flynn's to get new tennis balls, and there's no place to park our bikes there."

"May we go too?" Flossie asked.

"Of course we can go, silly," Freddie stated. "We're Bobbsey twins, too, like the ad said."

"Indeed you are!" Nan agreed. "You're in this just as much as Bert and I are."

As they drove through the Lakeport business district Flossie exclaimed, "Oh, what a lot of people! Why are there so many, Nan?"

"All the stores are having sales today," Nan answered. "But I've never seen the streets so crowded."

Soon Mr. Bobbsey drew up at the newspaper office. "Here you are," he said. "Don't get lost in the crowds."

After saying good-by to their father, the twins hopped out and went into the building. The girl in the ad department read Bert's notice and smiled.

"I have an Aunt Emma," she said. "But I'm sure she hasn't lost any money. I hope the right one sees your ad and gets hers back."

"We hope so too. Our ad will surely be in tomorrow morning's paper, won't it?" Nan asked, smiling back at her.

"I'll see to it," the girl promised.

The twins thanked her and went outside. Then

they headed for Flynn's Department Store where Bert wanted to buy the tennis balls. On the crowded street the children were jostled and pushed by the hurrying throngs.

"Flynn's is only a block from here," Bert said as he held tight to Freddie. "Hang onto Flossie, Nan."

His twin nodded. She kept Flossie's hand securely in hers.

"Flynn's must be making lots of money today," observed Freddie as they went into the store.

"I think everyone who isn't on the street is in here!" exclaimed Bert. "Where is the sports department, Nan?"

"Over to the right near the entrance," Nan told him. "But can we get there?" She laughed.

The twins made their way slowly to the counter where tennis balls were sold. Freddie and Flossie wandered away a few feet to watch a man who was buying a big rubber frog for his swimming pool.

The twins were so absorbed in the sale of the rubber frog that they did not notice a commotion down the aisle in which they were standing. Suddenly someone bumped into Flossie with such force that she was knocked to the floor.

"Oh!" she cried, as she struggled to get up. "Who hit me?"

Freddie was staring after the person who had run into Flossie.

"It was an old lady," he said. "Look! She's just going out the door." He helped Flossie to her feet in time to see the woman run outside.

Just then the twins heard a voice shout, "Stop her! Stop that old woman! She's a thief!" They could see a man pushing his way through the crowd in the aisle.

Nearly everyone, including the clerk who was waiting on Bert, hurried to see the excitement.

"She must have been a shoplifter," said a woman standing near by. "That was the store manager after her."

"What's a shoplifter?" Freddie asked the woman.

"A person who steals things from counters or racks," Freddie was told.

Another woman remarked, "I hear that Flynn's has been having a bad time lately with shoplifters."

A man standing next to Bert, who was holding a can of tennis balls, said, "The town seems to be full of them."

Just then a familiar voice behind Bert called out, "That's right. And Flynn's clerks had better watch out or they may have some tennis balls stolen!"

The twins recognized the voice as that of Danny Rugg. Danny was in Bert's grade and delighted in making trouble for the other children.

Bert grew red with anger. Everyone turned

to stare at him, and he looked as embarrassed as though he *had* intended to steal the tennis balls. Bert wanted to land his fist squarely in Danny's face, but his good sense told him not to start a fight in Flynn's store.

"Danny Rugg, you are the most *impossible* boy!" Nan cried indignantly. "Can't you ever be fair?"

Danny merely grinned. As the clerk came hurrying back to take Bert's money, the disagreeable boy sneered, "Had to pay for them, didn't you, Bertie boy?"

This was too much for Freddie. He marched directly up to Danny and planted his foot heavily on one of the bully's sneakers. Since Freddie was wearing sturdy, heavy-soled shoes, it was not a happy moment for Danny Rugg!

"Why, you little—" he began in a loud, angry voice. Then he saw the clerk at the tennis ball counter looking at him severely.

"Young fellow," the man said, "you seem to be a troublemaker. You'd better leave before I call the manager." Danny slunk away.

After buying the tennis balls, the twins left the store. They walked down the main street toward home with Nan and Bert keeping tight hold of the younger twins' hands.

Suddenly Freddie stopped short. "Oh!" he gasped. "Did you see that, Bert? A man grabbed that lady's purse!"

"Where?" Bert asked, staring around him.

Before Freddie could answer there was a shriek: "I've been robbed! Police!"

There was more pushing and crowding as everyone tried to see what was happening. A policeman came running up.

"Did anyone see the thief?" he asked.

"Yes!" shouted both Freddie and Flossie.

"What did he look like?" the officer asked.

"He was a big man with red hair—" Freddie began.

"Oh, no, Freddie," his twin interrupted. "I saw a lady in a blue dress take the money!"

"It was a man. I saw him as plain as I see you, Flossie," insisted Freddie.

"Well, which was it?" the officer asked. "I'll take the man with red hair. Did you see which way he went, sonny?"

The excited little boy pointed toward the south. "He was going that way, but he got mixed in with all the people."

The policeman hurried away into the crowd. As he disappeared another officer came from the other direction.

"What's going on here?" he asked. "More purse snatching?"

This time it was Flossie's turn. "I saw a blue lady in a yellow dress—no, I mean a lady in a blue dress with bright yellow hair take money out of another lady's handbag. She had a blue nose—I mean a big, funny-looking nose."

The policeman seemed confused. "A blue lady in a big dress with a yellow nose," he repeated, and then grinned.

"She went into that place between those two stores," Flossie added. Then, as the officer turned away still chuckling, the little girl faced Nan with tears in her blue eyes. "No one believes me," she said, "but I did see her."

"The policeman believes you, honey," Nan told her. "See? He's going into the alleyway between the buildings now."

"Oh! He is, isn't he?" exclaimed Flossie.

"Let's go watch this," Bert said.

The four children made their way to the dark passageway which led between the stores to an open space in the rear.

CHAPTER III

BERT'S PUZZLE

NO ONE was in sight, and Nan suggested that perhaps the children should go back through the alley and wait on the sidewalk for the policeman.

"There's the other officer," said Bert, as they came to the street.

He walked up to the twins. "I didn't see any red-haired man," he told Freddie. "Are you sure you saw one, buddy?"

"Yes, sir, I did," Freddie replied. "I guess he got away in a hurry."

The policeman gazed at the throngs of people walking or standing near them. "It's easy for purse snatchers to get away in such crowds," he said.

Footsteps in the alleyway set Flossie's heart beating hard. Was the lady thief coming? But only the officer walked out.

"Hi, Mike!" he said, greeting the other policeman. "Caught anyone yet?" Then he turned to Flossie. "No one was back there but an old woman hobbling along with a big basket."

At that moment a shriek rang out from the crowd. "My purse is open, and all my money is gone!" cried a woman, who was wearing a large black hat. She ran toward the policemen. Another woman, who wore a white hat, hurried after her.

Suddenly Flossie exclaimed, "The lady in the black hat! She's the one who had her money stolen by the mean lady in the blue dress with the big nose!"

The woman heard the little girl. "You saw someone open my purse and take out the money?" she asked.

"Yes, and she ran down that alley," Flossie answered. "I saw her take the money, and my twin saw a man grab another lady's purse."

"This is the lady right here," Freddie spoke up, pointing to the woman in the white hat.

"He's right," said the woman. The policeman who had heard her cry out when the thief took her bag agreed.

"We're sisters," said the woman in the white hat. "I'm Mrs. Hart. My sister is Mrs. Rudd. We were shopping together. I didn't find out until a few minutes ago that my money had been taken."

Policeman Mike patted Flossie's shoulder. "I'm afraid we didn't quite believe this little girl's story at first, but apparently it's true. Now we'll try very hard to find those two thieves."

"Indeed we will," the other officer said. "Evidently the shoplifters and purse snatchers are working in pairs. A red-haired man and a big-nosed woman."

He wrote down the two sisters' names in a book and said, "We'll call you ladies if we locate your stolen property."

The officers moved off. Mrs. Hart and Mrs. Rudd thanked the small twins for their help, then went on down the street.

"Let's go home," Nan said to Bert. "We can catch this next bus if we hurry."

"We'd *better* hurry before somebody steals our money," Freddie said, as they ran to the bus stop.

While riding along, Bert asked Flossie to tell him about the thief in the blue dress. "Just what did she look like?"

"Ugh! She had a funny-looking big nose, and her eyes were squinted, and her face was like this." Flossie stretched the skin on her round cheeks until her blue eyes were nearly closed.

The others laughed. "She must have been a beauty," observed Bert. "I wish I'd seen her."

Lunch was ready when the twins reached home. Their father, who took Saturday afternoons off, was waiting for them. "I might have known you'd have an adventure," he said after they told about the morning's excitement. "When anything happens, the Bobbsey twins are always on the spot!"

"That's what Charlie says," Bert remarked, laughing. Charlie Mason was his best friend.

"Speaking of Charlie, how would you like to ask him to help you with the experiment?" Mr. Bobbsey asked, his eyes twinkling.

"Hot diggity, Dad! Does this mean you've heard something?" Bert exclaimed.

"I talked to John Harper this morning," his father replied. "He thinks it's a fine idea."

"Now can we know the secret?" Nan asked pleadingly.

Mr. Bobbsey smiled. "Tell them, Bert."

As the others listened eagerly, Bert said, "We're going to camp on Mr. Harper's property on Blueberry Island for a week, starting Monday."

"Oh, how wonderful!" Nan exclaimed.

Freddie yelled, "Yippee!" and Flossie squealed, "Um, that's scrumptious!"

"I'm going to make a trial labyrinth on Blueberry Island," Bert said.

"A trial what?" asked Freddie, mystified.

Bert explained that a labyrinth was a maze, a series of crisscrossed paths between walls or high hedges. It was a kind of game, and the object was for a person to try to find his way into the center of the maze and out again. This was not easy to do, as many of the paths had no exit, and then the person would have to go back and start all over again.

"Haven't you noticed the funny-looking designs I've been making on paper lately?" Bert asked. "Mr. Tetlow, our school principal, saw my last design, and he said I might make a maze for the school fair this fall. We can make money by charging admission and giving a prize to anyone who guesses the key."

"What key?" asked Freddie.

"The secret of how you get into the center of the maze and out again is called the key," Bert explained.

He said that in olden days gardens were made in the form of labyrinths on the huge estates of kings. The paths were laid out in such a mixed-up pattern that no one could reach the center unless he knew the secret, or key.

"Do you know the key to your maze?" Freddie asked his brother.

"Of course I do, because I made the design for it." Bert laughed.

"Oh, show us, show us!" Flossie begged, jumping up and down happily.

"I'd rather let you try to find out yourself," Bert told her. "It would spoil the fun to show you the plan."

"That's right," said Mr. Bobbsey. "But I think your maze will be more diffiult to build than to design on paper. Also, you'll have only about a week to do it. But with Charlie to help and Sam to cut the brush, I think you can make it."

"Why do you need brushes?" Flossie asked.

"The idea," said Bert, laughing, "is to have high hedges on each side of the paths. On Blueberry Island the bushes are already there. Sam will cut through some of them to make the paths."

"Neat," said Freddie.

Nan offered to help build the maze, and Bert nodded. Then Mrs. Bobbsey asked Nan if she would help locate the family's camping clothes. "I'm afraid some of them are pretty well worn or outgrown," she said.

"I'll help you, Mother," Nan replied. "It'll be fun just to see them again. Is all the camp stuff up in the attic?" Her mother nodded.

Mr. Bobbsey said he thought they would need new tents. "Ours are too old to be serviceable. I'll check the equipment," he offered.

"I'll tell Charlie the good news," Bert said as soon as lunch was over.

He left, and Mr. Bobbsey soon followed him out of the house. Mrs. Bobbsey and Nan went up to the attic, and the younger twins were left alone in the living room.

Freddie went over to the wastebasket and came

back with a piece of paper. "Here's a drawing of a maze Bert isn't going to use," he said. "Let's go make one in the back yard."

"All right," Flossie agreed with enthusiasm.

They ran out the side door and went directly to the garage to get the big clippers. Freddie laid the labyrinth design on the grass, then picked up the shears to cut off some of the hedge. He had

trouble managing the clippers but finally did cut off a large section of privet hedge.

"We'll make the maze under the cherry tree," he told his twin. "I'll dig holes, and we can stick the branches in."

"Oh, that's bee-oo-ti-ful!" Flossie said admiringly as her brother put the green twigs into the ground.

Freddie went to clip another hunk out of the hedge. "It does look nice," he added after he had stuck that in too. "I'll get some more."

When he came back with the next cutting he saw that a sprig of flowers had been added to the maze. "It looks prettier with flowers," Flossie said. "I got them from the garden."

"Bert doesn't have flowers in his picture," Freddie objected. He started to pull out the blossoms.

"Freddie Bobbsey! Stop that!" cried Flossie.

Nan had come down to look for the little twins and heard Flossie's voice. She hurried toward the garden. "Flossie! Freddie! Mother wants you to try on— Ooh!"

The twins knew by the tone of Nan's voice that they had been naughty.

"We are making a labo—labo—oh, a maze." Freddie tried to defend himself.

"You've gone and cut pieces out of our nice hedge. It looks terrible!" Nan cried in dismay.

"Sam cut pieces off the top yesterday," Flossie informed her. "I saw him."

"That's different. Sam knows how to trim it," Nan said. Then she saw their ashamed faces and added, "Maybe Sam can fix up the hedge. But you mustn't use the clippers any more. You might have cut yourselves. Now, come on in. Mother wants you to try on your last year's camp clothes."

The younger twins scampered into the house with a last guilty look at the hedge.

The next morning Bert was up early and ran to the front porch for the newspaper. He brought it to the table where the rest of the family was just sitting down to breakfast.

"Look," Bert said. "Here's our ad."

Mr. Bobbsey took the paper and read the small advertisement. "That ought to bring an answer," he said. Then, turning to the front page, he exclaimed, "Listen to this! 'Because of the wave of shoplifting and purse snatching that has struck Lakeport within the past two weeks, the Citizens' League is offering a reward of five hundred dollars for the capture or information leading to the capture of the thieves.' "

"Boy, I'd like to win that reward!" Bert said. "But we'll be on Blueberry Island all next week, so I guess there's not much chance."

"I wish I'd grabbed that man I saw take the lady's purse!" Freddie groaned.

"I could have caught hold of the blue lady's dress," Flossie added.

"Let's go tell Susie Larker and Teddy Blake about the store thieves we saw yesterday morning," Freddie suggested to his twin. Susie and Teddy were Freddie's and Flossie's age, and were their constant playmates. When the twins phoned to see if the children would be home, Susie invited them over to spend the afternoon.

"Come home by five o'clock," Mrs. Bobbsey told them, when the two little twins started off.

Nan and Bert went to spend the afternoon with friends, too. All the twins started home near suppertime. Freddie was the first to arrive, with Flossie right behind him. Bert and Nan were a short distance down the block.

Freddie ran up the porch steps. "Last one in is a monkey!" he shouted. Then he saw a letter that was sticking out of the mailbox. "What's this?" he asked himself curiously, taking it out. "It hasn't any stamp, and it's printed sort of funny."

Nan and Bert had caught up with Flossie. All three gazed at the letter.

"Whose name is on it?" asked Nan.

Freddie examined the letter. "It's addressed to The Bobbsey Twins," he said. "You open it, Bert."

His brother tore open the envelope. "Well, for the love of Pete!" he exclaimed.

"What does it say?" Flossie demanded, looking at the smeared page on which the message was scrawled in crayon.

" 'Warning!' " Bert read aloud. " 'Put the money you found in a package under the big white birch tree by the bandstand tonight at eight o'clock, or you will be reported to the police as thieves!' "

CHAPTER IV

PLAYING TRICKS

"THIEVES! We're not thieves!" Flossie cried, stamping one foot in exasperation.

"Of course not," said Nan. "Anyway, the police have the money."

Freddie was staring at the letter. "The bandstand. That's in the park."

"Yes," Bert said. He had been rereading the letter. Finally he told the others he believed it was a joke. "The kind of joke Danny Rugg would play," he added thoughtfully.

"You're right," Nan agreed. "That would be just like Danny. And he probably read our ad in the paper this morning."

At this moment Mrs. Bobbsey came into the room. She was shown the note, and Bert told her his suspicions.

"I'd like to play a joke on Danny," he said, his eyes twinkling. "Okay, Mother?"

Mrs. Bobbsey smiled. "It depends on what the joke is," she said.

"I don't know yet. But I'll get Charlie Mason to help me." He started for the telephone.

Mrs. Bobbsey thought Dinah might have seen someone around. "Let's check with Dinah first," she suggested.

They all trooped to the kitchen where Sam's wife was just taking a baked ham from the oven.

"Umm! That smells delicious, Dinah!" Nan exclaimed.

The plump woman smiled broadly. "There sure is nothing like ham for a picnic, unless it's home-baked beans. I've got a big pot o' those in the oven too. You'll need a sight of eatables to take to Blueberry Island tomorrow."

"Dinah," said Mrs. Bobbsey, "did you see anyone on the porch while Mr. Bobbsey and I were out this afternoon?"

"Not exactly, Mrs. Bobbsey. I heard the mailbox top go flop, though. I knew it couldn't be the postman, so I went to look out the window. I saw a boy—he looked like that Rugg boy—running down the street like he had mad dogs chasin' him. Is there somethin' wrong, Mrs. Bobbsey?"

"There was a silly letter for the twins in the box," answered Mrs. Bobbsey. She turned to Bert. "Your guess was right. Go ahead and call up Charlie."

Soon Charlie Mason arrived. He was a tall,

well-built boy like Bert, with a wide, friendly smile. Charlie was a great favorite in the Bobbsey household. After they had greeted him in the living room, Charlie said to Mrs. Bobbsey, "It's swell of you and Mr. Bobbsey to ask me to go camping with you!"

"We'll enjoy having you, Charlie," she told him. "There should be a good chance for you and Bert to practice making the labyrinth on the island."

Nan asked him what he thought of the letter that had come.

"It's a trick of Danny Rugg's all right. And Bert and I have figured out how we can turn the tables on him."

"How?" asked Freddie eagerly.

"You tell them, Bert," Charlie suggested.

Bert took the toy money game from the top of the bookcase. "We'll use a bunch of these fake ten-dollar bills," he said. "We'll wrap them in a piece of newspaper and put them in this paper bag." He held up the bag for them to see. "Then we'll put this under the birch tree by the bandstand and wait to see who picks it up."

"Goody, goody!" Flossie cried out, clapping her hands. "That'll fool Danny."

Bert looked at Mrs. Bobbsey. "All right, Mother?"

She chuckled. "I hope you're right about

Danny. But if some strange man picks it up, don't let him see you. Get a good look at him and give his description to the police."

"We'd better go early," Charlie suggested. "There's a space under the bandstand where we can hide and watch the path by the birch tree."

"Good idea," said Bert. "Charlie, come by about seven-thirty. I'll be ready to go. Want to come along, Nan?"

"I'd love to," Nan said.

When seven-thirty came, Flossie and Freddie wanted to be included. Mr. Bobbsey said he would drive them to the park. But he and the younger twins would stay in the background in the car.

When Charlie arrived, Mr. Bobbsey drove to the entrance to the park and let the three older children out there. Bert laid the paper bag under the white birch tree, then he crawled into the dark space under the bandstand with Nan and Charlie.

It was about three minutes to eight by the near-by church tower clock when Charlie whispered hoarsely, "Someone's coming!"

In the dim light of the evening they saw an old woman walking slowly along the path. She wore a long skirt and a shawl that covered her head, shoulders, and arms. When she reached the birch tree, the woman stumbled slightly and

She bent to pick up the paper bag

lifted her skirt as she bent to pick up the paper bag.

"That's Danny!" whispered Bert. "I know those ink-spotted sneakers!"

He dived out with Nan and Charlie following him. Before the stooping figure could straighten up, Bert was upon it. He snatched off the black shawl and disclosed the frightened face of Danny Rugg.

"Look out!" cried Nan. "Here come his friends!"

Two boys who had been lurking in the background ran toward them, fists extended.

"It's Jack Westley and Peewee Morse," Charlie said, squaring off. "I can handle them, Bert, if you'll take care of Danny."

Bert was already "taking care" of Danny, who was somewhat hampered by his long skirt.

"Danny Rugg, I have a score to settle with you!" Bert stormed, as he thrust his fist into Danny's jaw.

"Let me go, Bert Bobbsey!" screamed Danny. He made a pass at Bert's face.

Bert dodged and brought his fist toward Danny's chest. But halfway he stopped. "*Mrs.* Danny Rugg," he said, "I'll wait until you take off that costume before I hit you again. Hurry! Get it off!"

Instead of removing it, Danny gathered up his skirt and ran down the path. His friends, who were getting the worst of the battle with Charlie, hurried to follow him.

"Let them go," said Nan, giggling. "They know they're beaten."

The fleeing boys, listening for footsteps behind them, instead heard peals of laughter. To make it worse, as they left the park they met Mr. Bobbsey and the younger twins.

Flossie and Freddie burst out laughing "Oh, Danny Rugg, you look so funny!" Freddie yelled.

Looking miserable, Danny put on speed. He and his friends disappeared around a corner.

Mr. Bobbsey glanced after them, chuckling. "I think Danny has had a mighty uncomfortable evening," he remarked.

Nan and the two boys came out of the park, still laughing. "Here's your money," Bert said, handing the bag to Flossie. "It wasn't even touched."

"I wonder what Danny Rugg will do to get even with us for this evening," Nan said, as Mr. Bobbsey drove off.

"You never can tell," Bert replied cheerfully. "We'll just have to keep one jump ahead of him."

They let Charlie out at his house and then went home. As Bert closed the garage door for his father, Mr. Bobbsey said, "Sam's taking a load of camping equipment to the launch first thing in the morning. Do you want to go with him, son?"

"Yes, Dad, and I think it's super that we're to have the *Tall Timber* at the island."

"It will be a real necessity for me," his father replied. "I'll have to come back to the office at least twice while we're there."

Bert was up early next morning to help Sam put the equipment into the station wagon. There were new tents, sleeping bags, rubber mattresses, a big folding grill and numerous hampers of cooking utensils and supplies.

"Sakes alive!" exclaimed Sam, chuckling. "That's enough gear for a month o' Sundays!"

It was still early when they drew up at the lumberyard dock. The lake was a deep, sparkling blue.

"Here are the fishing rods and stuff," Bert said as he pulled the long, slender cases out of the car. "I hope we're lucky and catch some big trout."

"Or a bass or pickerel," Sam grinned as they stowed their load.

"What's this funny-looking saw?" Bert asked, as the tool was put aboard. "It looks like a saber."

"That's what it's called," Sam said. "A saber-saw. Your father tells me you want a lot of branches and stuff cut for that maze you're goin' to make. This saw's a whiz for cuttin' those things."

"Great!" said Bert.

At that moment a small outboard motorboat roared past the end of the dock. Bert noticed that there were two people aboard, but he could not see them plainly. The one nearer him, a man, wore a light raincoat and pulled-down hat. Almost as soon as the boat was out of sight, the sound of the motor stopped.

Sam scratched his head, a puzzled expression on his face. "Wonder where that boat docked?" he muttered. "I don't know any landin' place near here."

"Maybe it tied up to a tree along the shore," Bert suggested, grinning.

They went on with their work and soon finished stowing everything on the *Tall Timber*. As they drove home, Bert explained to Sam why he wanted to construct the maze. Then he told him about the ones made long ago for kings and queens.

"Gracious!" exclaimed Sam, laughing. "Seems like a powerful lot o' work just to get folks mixed up!"

Bert laughed too. "It's like making a puzzle on a big scale. Everyone likes a puzzle, Sam."

"I know that, but I'm not much on figurin' things out, Bert. I'll just cut the brush and haul it for you and Charlie. I'll let you do all the puzzlin'." Sam grinned. "While you're doin' it, I'll go fishin'."

As they reached the house, the postman was coming along the street. He handed a letter to Bert. "I see by the paper that you found some money," he said. "I think I've brought your first answer to the ad."

Bert thanked him and carried the letter into the house. "Something for the Bobbsey twins," he called out.

Nan, Flossie, and Freddie came running to see what it was.

"You open this one, Nan," Bert said, handing it over.

Nan took a paper knife from the desk and slit the envelope carefully. "Oh!" she cried. "Listen to this! It's from a lady who lives on Blueberry Island, where we're going!"

CHAPTER V

THE OLD SHACK

"IS THE letter from 'Aunt Emma?' " Flossie asked excitedly.

"Yes, it is," Nan replied. "Let's read it at the breakfast table."

The twins hurried into the dining room where Mr. and Mrs. Bobbsey were already seated.

"Hurry up, Nan," Flossie begged.

Nan said the letter was written in pencil and was hard to read. "So I can't go very fast. Here it is:

" 'Bobbsey twins, the money you found is mine. My niece lost it on the 24th of June. Please bring it to me or send it because I am lame and cannot get around. I live on the north end of Blueberry Island in the 4th cabin. You have to go through the woods. Mrs. Emma Whiteside.' "

"Poor old lady!" Mrs. Bobbsey exclaimed. "She must be all alone out there on the island."

Flossie looked worried. "Let's get the money from the p'lice and take it right out to her," she urged.

"First we have to get some proof," Bert spoke up. "Mrs. Whiteside doesn't give us any. We said in the ad that whoever claimed the money must show proof."

Mr. Bobbsey nodded. "That's right, son. The pack of ten-dollar bills was evidently fresh from a bank. She should be able to tell us which bank it was, and we could check there." At this moment Dinah came in with a plate of blueberry corn cake. As she set it on the table Nan said laughingly, "While we're on Blueberry Island, and Dinah's here, who'll make all the blueberry pies and muffins?"

"There'll be no baking at camp," her mother declared, smiling. "But if the berries are ripe on the island we can bring plenty home with us."

"I reckon I'll have to bake you considerable cookies to take along," Dinah said, chuckling. "When are you all leavin'?"

"After lunch," the twins' mother replied.

Mr. Bobbsey unfolded the morning paper and began to read it. "Here's another article about the series of robberies that are sweeping the town," he said. "The police are warning everyone to be on guard and to watch for sneak thieves. They ask people to report any suspicious-looking strangers."

"Such as Flossie's yellow lady in the big dress with the blue nose?" Bert teased, as his father paused.

Flossie made a face at her older brother. "Well, I did see a funny-looking lady take money out of that Mrs. Rudd's purse," she said.

Mr. Bobbsey went on, "Besides the purse snatching and shoplifting, there have been two house robberies. Police warn us to keep doors and windows locked when no one is at home."

"We'd better tell Dinah to be extra careful," Nan said worriedly. "She won't have Snap here to bark at strangers."

"Maybe Snoop can meow extra loud," Freddie said hopefully.

As the family started to separate after breakfast, Mrs. Bobbsey said, "Lunch will be at twelve, so we can leave before one. Bert, why don't you invite Charlie to lunch?"

"I'll go ask him now. He can bring his things over here this morning. I'll help him carry them." Bert hurried out of the house.

During the morning the rest of the camp equipment was stowed in the station wagon. It was crammed full. A little before one o'clock Charlie and the family climbed in. Flossie and Freddie had to sit on Nan's and Bert's laps.

Freddie laughed. "We look like a moving van that takes people too!"

"And dogs," added Flossie, gazing at Snap,

who was perched on a suitcase near the roof.

When they pulled up to the boathouse at the lumberyard, Sam met them. Bert and Freddie helped him put most of the baggage aboard the *Tall Timber.* The overflow was stowed in a rowboat attached to the stern.

Meanwhile, Flossie pulled at Nan's sweater sleeve. "A man over there is watching us. See? He's on the other side of that pile of lumber."

Nan looked just in time to see a man disappear from view outside the yard. "That's funny," she thought.

"Everybody aboard!" called Mr. Bobbsey after Sam had driven the station wagon into the garage at the lumberyard.

As the launch started away, with Sam at the wheel, a small outboard motorboat sped past them. The pilot, who was alone, wore a light raincoat and a pulled-down hat.

"That's the same man who was peeking at us," Flossie declared.

Nan shaded her eyes and stared after him, as Bert remarked, "Sam and I saw him this morning. He certainly whips up a lot of speed from that little motor."

"I think it spoils a ride to go so fast," Mrs. Bobbsey said. "I like Sam's steady pace better."

When they reached deeper water, Freddie asked, "Please may we go around a lot of the islands before we go to Blueberry?"

The others agreed, and the launch cruised along the channels between the wooded spots. Nan kept looking for the curious stranger, but did not see him again. Finally the *Tall Timber* headed for Blueberry Island.

"Let's go see Mrs. Whiteside first, Daddy," Nan said. "Oh, I hope the poor old lady can remember which bank paid the money to her niece."

As the *Tall Timber* headed for the north end of the island, Mr. Bobbsey took out the binoculars. They were kept in a locker near the pilot's seat in the little cabin. After looking through them, he said, "I think I see a dock up there."

Sam steered for the spot. There was a ramshackle pier in a small inlet. Near it, on a cleared strip of land, stood three shabby, unpainted houses. Two of them seemed to be vacant with boarded-up windows and wild grapes growing almost to the doorsteps. The third cabin, however, had crisp curtains in the windows. Pots of pink geraniums adorned the broken-down porch.

"Does Mrs. Whiteside live there?" Flossie asked.

"We'll find out," her mother replied.

She and the twins stepped out of the launch and went up to the cabin. In answer to Mrs. Bobbsey's knock the door was opened by a young, tired-looking woman. Two little children clung to her skirt. Mrs. Bobbsey introduced herself and the twins and said they were looking for a Mrs. Whiteside.

"My name is Turner—Mrs. John Turner," the young woman said. "I don't know anyone named Whiteside. But there's a cabin a distance through the woods. I think it has occupants now, but I'm not sure what their name is. Follow the path to your right and you'll find it."

Snap was wagging his tail and evidently wanted to play with the little children. They laughed and patted his head.

"Do you have any other children, Mrs. Turner?" Nan asked.

A smile brightened the young woman's wan face. "Yes, I have an older son who is ten. He is a great help to me in every way since his father died. Tommy earns quite a bit of money picking and selling the wild blueberries that grow on the island."

"I'd like to do that," said Freddie.

"And give up being a fireman?" Flossie teased him. Her twin preferred playing with toy fire equipment to all other games.

Mrs. Bobbsey thanked Mrs. Turner for her information and told her they were going to camp on the south end of the island. She called Mr. Bobbsey and Sam, and the whole group started off through the woods of stunted oak and pine.

A young fawn dashed out of the woods

"How dark it's growing!" exclaimed Mrs. Bobbsey, glancing at the sky. "I hope it doesn't rain."

"I think the sun's just resting his eyes behind a big cloud," Flossie observed after she had studied the cloud-swept arc above her. But as she hurried along, the little girl remarked, "Oo, it's dark and spooky in these woods!"

The underbrush crowded the path so thickly that the group had to walk single file. There was no conversation for a while, then Nan spoke up. "I can't help wishing that the money we found belonged to Mrs. Turner. I feel so sorry for her."

Before anyone could answer, there was a sudden crashing of branches close beside them. A young fawn dashed out of the woods, nearly bumping into Flossie.

"Oh!" she cried out.

But the fawn seemed even more startled than Flossie and with another leap disappeared into the woods on the other side of the path.

"What a d-darling deer!" the little girl gasped after she had caught her breath.

Bert turned to Charlie, who was just behind him, and said in a low voice, "I wonder what frightened that fawn to make it run out in front of us. It was going so fast it didn't hear us."

"I think there's someone or something in the woods near by who is keeping pace with us, Bert," Charlie murmured softly. "I've been hearing the bushes crackle every once in a while."

"So have I," Bert replied. "I wonder why he doesn't come out in the open."

As they walked on, both boys listened and watched for further evidence of the mysterious person in the woods. They saw no one but heard the same stealthy sounds of stirring branches. Snap kept running off the path, but since he did not bark, the boys were not alarmed.

Finally Mr. Bobbsey, in the lead, reached a clearing. "There's the cabin," he called back and then waited for the others to catch up with him.

The building was little more than a shack, which stood among trees beside the water. A dilapidated boathouse near by was almost hidden by trees and shrubbery.

"Nobody's here," Freddie said. "There are boards over the windows."

"It does look deserted," Mr. Bobbsey agreed. "But I'll knock on the door anyway."

"Look at Snap!" cried Flossie suddenly.

The shaggy white fur at the back of Snap's neck was standing up in an odd way, and he was growling softly. Sam snapped the leash on the dog's collar.

"Mr. Snap don't like this place," he said. "He's mighty suspicious about the folks that's been around here."

Mr. Bobbsey had stepped onto the rickety porch and was knocking on the door. There was no answer. He knocked again.

Bert still had a feeling that there was someone in the woods behind him. He turned quickly to look back at the path which they had traveled. No one was in sight, but he noticed that the leaves of a low tree at the edge of the path were moving violently. There was no wind, so someone must have disturbed them!

"I'll send Snap to find out what's going on," Bert decided.

Just then there came an answer to Mr. Bobbsey's knock. "Open the door and walk in," a voice called. It was cracked and hoarse.

Mr. Bobbsey lifted the iron latch and pushed at the door which stuck slightly, then opened on creaking hinges. The room inside was dim.

Snap was growling, so Sam kept him out on the porch while the others went inside. Then he followed, holding Snap close beside him on the leash.

"Well!" said the hoarse voice sharply, "did the whole town come?"

As their eyes became accustomed to the dimness, the Bobbseys knew that the words had been spoken by an old woman in a wheelchair. She was so far back in a dark corner that they could barely see her face. A few pieces of old furniture were scattered about the room, and some luggage was piled against the walls. Articles of clothing spilled untidily from it.

Mr. Bobbsey introduced himself and the others, but the woman did not give her name.

"Well," she snapped in her unpleasant voice, "If you're the Bobbsey twins, where is my money?"

CHAPTER VI

UNFRIENDLY ISLANDERS

WHEN THE callers did not answer the old lady, she asked which ones were the Bobbsey twins. Bert and Nan stepped forward, with the younger twins close behind them.

"We are the Bobbsey twins, Mrs. Whiteside," Bert answered. "All of our family and Sam and my friend Charlie Mason are going to camp for a week on the other side of the island."

"You don't say!" exclaimed Mrs. Whiteside.

All this time Flossie had been looking around the room. She pulled at her twin's sleeve. "Look, Freddie," she whispered, "those windows over there are all covered up with boards so no light can come in. Why do you s'pose she wants it so dark in here?"

"Maybe her eyes hurt or something," Freddie replied. Then as he looked around the room he added, "Maybe the place is so mussed up she doesn't want anyone to see it."

"I guess that's it," Flossie agreed.

Mrs. Whiteside could not hear what the younger twins were saying because she was talking in loud, angry tones. "That money is mine," she cried, "and I want it back!"

"How much money was in the package you lost?" Bert asked her.

"Five hundred dollars," replied the old lady quickly. "It was marked so on the purple band around it."

"There wasn't that much in the stack that we found, Mrs. Whiteside," Bert told her. "Some had been taken out."

"What! Oh, that wicked girl!" wailed Mrs. Whiteside loudly. "How much did she steal before she lost all my money?"

"What girl?" Nan asked.

"Why, my niece."

Snap had been watching anxiously as the children went farther into the room. Suddenly he pricked up his ears and turned his attention to a closed door which evidently led to another room in the shack.

Charlie was standing near it and tried to see what had attracted Snap's interest. He saw nothing, but heard a faint sound as though someone had brushed against the other side of the loosely hung door.

Mr. Bobbsey spoke before Bert could answer the old lady's question. "I'm afraid you'll have to show some proof that the money belongs to you, Mrs. Whiteside," he said gently.

"I told you how much was there before my niece stole some of it. I told you about the purple band around it. What more do you want to know?" she demanded.

"If you will give us the name of your bank, we can check on the withdrawal," Mr. Bobbsey explained.

"Oh, my memory is too bad to remember that," the old lady whined. "The money is mine by rights, so please give it to me now."

"There's a special way to tell if it's your money," Freddie piped up helpfully. "Was it in a package with anything else?"

Mrs. Whiteside apparently did not hear the question. She gave her chair an impatient shove from its corner. "Pen!" she called in a surprisingly strong voice. "Pen! Come here!"

"Oh, look!" gasped Freddie, pointing.

The wheelchair had touched a long iron pipe which had been placed against the shadowy wall behind Mrs. Whiteside. It was sliding as Freddie spoke, and now it fell with a bang, just escaping one of the boarded-up windows.

There was an eerie rattling and bumping in the rafters overhead. Then, as everyone stared up into cobwebby darkness, a huge bat swept down. Its wings barely missed Nan's head. She ducked quickly, and Flossie shrieked.

Sam opened the door onto the porch. Bert and Charlie, with Mr. Bobbsey, tried to drive the flying creature out.

In the midst of the confusion the door which Snap had been watching opened. A man came out, carrying a broom. He was large and stooped, and his clothes hung loosely on him.

"Get it, Pen!" the old woman cackled. "Hurry, son!"

Pen raised his arms. With a quick sweep he caught the bat in mid-air and swept it outdoors. Snap was growling and pulling at his leash, but Sam held him firmly.

"Shut the door!" commanded the old lady.

Sam closed it, and Nan bent to pat Snap's head lovingly.

Flossie, who had hid her face in her mother's skirt when the bat was flying about, whispered, "Can't we go?"

"Very soon, dear."

Mrs. Whiteside said in a complaining voice, "Pen, make these people give me my money."

Mr. Bobbsey spoke before the man could answer. "You must realize, sir, that we'll need proof that Mrs. Whiteside is the rightful owner before the money can be turned over to her."

"My mother don't need proof. You'd better give up that wad of bills with no more talk, mister," Pen Whiteside said in an ugly voice. He kept his head down and turned away from Mr. Bobbsey as he spoke.

Mr. Bobbsey motioned for Sam to open the door. As the callers went outside, he turned to the old lady. "We'll be at the south end of the island for a week. If you can produce evidence the money is yours, I'll see that you get it. Good day, Mrs. Whiteside."

Her son looked as if he would like to start a fight, but after gazing at Mr. Bobbsey, the two husky boys, stalwart Sam, and the growling dog, he apparently changed his mind. This was evidently too much for one man to tackle alone.

Instead, Pen said pleasantly, "The money came from a bank out of town. I don't know as I can get any kind of proof."

"Let me know when you do," Mr. Bobbsey replied.

There was no answer as Pen Whiteside slammed the door shut.

"What a shifty-eyed character he is!" Bert exclaimed, as he followed Charlie along the path. "And say, I saw a leaf and a dried twig caught in the cuff of his trouser leg. Do you think he could be the man we heard in the woods?"

"Sure," Charlie replied. "He must have climbed in through a window in that next room after we were inside the cabin. What a creep!"

"How different the Turner cabin is from the

one we just visited!" Mrs. Bobbsey remarked.

"The Whitesides' place is certainly a sight!" Nan exclaimed.

"I don't like that old lady," Flossie declared. "That was an awful dirty house."

"I s'pose she can't get out of the wheelchair to clean and sweep," Freddie said, "but that man could help her."

"I wonder why Mrs. Whiteside's son couldn't have come to Lakeport for the money," Nan remarked. "I thought from what she said in the letter that she lived alone."

"I thought of that too, Nan," her father said. "There's something odd about it."

Soon the Bobbseys came out of the woods. The sun had by now emerged from the clouds and shone full and bright.

"I'll race you boys to the dock!" Nan called out. The three started off at top speed, with the younger twins racing along behind them. Snap joined the contest and was soon leaping ahead.

"Hurry up, Nan!" urged Flossie. "Bert's going to win!" cried Freddie. "Hurray for Bert!"

"Snap really won," said Flossie, and this was true.

Sam stepped into the launch and soon had the motor purring softly. Bert looked at the rowboat being towed by the *Tall Timber* and carrying extra equipment. "May Charlie and I ride in the dinghy, Dad?" he asked.

His father regarded the small boat thoughtfully. "It's pretty well loaded, Bert. You may ship some water."

"We won't mind that, will we, Charlie?" Bert asked.

"It's a warm day," Charlie said, laughing. "A shower bath might feel good."

"You'll have to squeeze in among the canvas tents and duffle bags," Mr. Bobbsey told them.

The two boys stepped into the rowboat and slid in under the cargo. As the *Tall Timber* left the dock a small wave slapped over the prow of the rowboat.

"I'm glad this stuff is waterproof," Bert said.

"And I'm glad I am." Charlie chuckled.

The boat was very low in the water. As Sam steered along the shore it received the full force of the back wash from the *Tall Timber*. But the boys enjoyed it.

The southern end of Blueberry Island looked very wild and beautiful. The banks were high and covered with shrubbery, so those in the boats could see very little of the land.

Freddie peered through the binoculars. "Do you see any bears?" Flossie asked him.

"No, maybe they're behind all the bushes."

"Bears don't live on these islands, my little sweet fairy," Mr. Bobbsey said, smiling.

"They like blueberries so much they might come to this one—" she began.

"Oh!" exclaimed Nan suddenly. "Look at the rowboat, Daddy!"

The waves from the launch were almost swamping the dinghy as it rose and fell.

"Slow down, Sam!" Mr. Bobbsey called. Sam cut down speed at once. Smiling, he said, "We're almost to the cove now where we're goin' to land."

"Let me steer for a minute, Daddy," Freddie begged.

"Not now, little fireman," Mr. Bobbsey replied. "Those big rocks you see on shore extend under the water too. We need an experienced pilot here."

"Daddy!" cried Freddie. "I forgot my fire pumper! What if we have a fire at camp!"

"I guess we'll just have to be extra careful,"

his father answered. Then as the *Tall Timber* rounded a point of land, he added, "Here we are!"

They were in a small harbor with a wooded, rocky coast on three sides. A narrow strip of beach marked the landing place. Sam anchored the launch about twenty feet from shore. From here the campers would be taken ashore in the dinghy after it was unloaded.

Bert called out, "Dad, Charlie and I are so wet that we may as well swim ashore. Okay?"

"Okay," his father replied, chuckling.

Bert and Charlie dived into the water. They swam rapidly to the beach, then ran up and down the sand in the sun.

"That rowboat ride was almost like water-skiing," Charlie said, laughing, to Mr. Bobbsey as he and Sam landed with the first load of supplies.

"The tents got mighty wet," Sam observed. "But it won't take long to dry 'em out."

Bert and Charlie offered to unpack and hang up the sodden equipment.

As they worked, Charlie suddenly said, "Bert, maybe Pen Whiteside has an idea your dad has that money here with him. Do you think he might come to camp after dark and try to find it?"

CHAPTER VII

BUILDING A MAZE

WHEN Charlie asked Bert the question about Pen Whiteside, Bert looked thoughtful. "He'd be taking a chance on getting Snap's teeth in his leg," he replied. "But that guy looks mean enough to try 'most anything."

The rowboat arrived just then with the rest of the Bobbseys, and the boys hurried to help Sam pull it up on the beach.

"Isn't this beautiful!" exclaimed Mrs. Bobbsey as she stepped onto the sand.

"Um! It smells good too," Flossie said, sniffing the sweet fern and pine odors of the woods.

"It's only a short walk through the grove to camp," Mr. Bobbsey told them. "If everyone will carry something that's dry, Sam and the boys and I will come back for the wet things later."

It did not take long to reach the stretch of open

ground where the camp was to be set up. A level space high above the water offered an ideal place for the tents.

The entire clearing was about one hundred feet square and hedged in on three sides with a thick growth of stunted pine, scrub oaks, and bushes. Along the shore the bank was rimmed with tall rank-growing shrubs which practically hid the lake from view.

Beyond the clearing to the north stood an enormous oak tree. It rose from a tangle of shrubbery and underbrush.

"That tree looks like a lighthouse," remarked Freddie.

Bert gazed at the tree with shining eyes. "It will make a keen center for our labyrinth, Charlie!" he exclaimed. "That thicket on this side looks about the size I planned for this end of the maze. We can cut the paths right out of the underbrush."

"You bet!" Charlie agreed. "Come on, let's bring the rest of the equipment and set up the tents. Then we can go to work on your labyrinth."

Inside of an hour the camp was established. "Wow, this is some place!" exclaimed Charlie, looking at the trim colony of five tents. "Who sleeps where?"

Mr. Bobbsey answered. "The girls have one

of the larger tents. Mrs. Bobbsey and I have another. Sam and Freddie each have a small one. The largest tent is for housekeeping and storage purposes."

"You and I have sleeping bags, Charlie," Bert told his friend. "We can sleep where we like."

"There are a couple of pup tents for any emergencies, such as rain or extra guests," Mr. Bobbsey added.

Charlie grinned. "Snap should have a pup tent," he joked. Then he added, "What is Sam doing?"

"He's unfolding the self-inflating mattresses," Bert said.

"You sure have all the latest in camp stuff," Charlie remarked admiringly.

Snap had been bounding about inspecting the strange new place. He ran ahead of Bert and Nan as they walked with Charlie across the clearing.

"Hot diggity!" exclaimed Bert. "Look at all those blueberry bushes. They'll be perfect for the maze!" He drew a paper from his pocket and spread it out. "Here's the design," he added.

The maze was twice as long as it was wide and was filled with twisting paths.

"Plenty of blind alleys to fool people," Charlie remarked, chuckling.

As the two boys studied the design, Nan began

to make her way through the tangled underbrush. It tore at her clothes and whipped her face.

"These bushes hide the whole lower part of the tree trunk from this side," she remarked to herself. "I wonder if it's as thick on the other side."

Suddenly the boys heard her shout. "Bert! Charlie! There are bushes everywhere except on the north side!"

"No bushes!" Bert exclaimed. "I wonder why."

He and Charlie forced their way through the thicket to join Nan. She was seated on a wide tree stump which stood close to a giant oak. In front of her was a large cleared space.

"That stump looks freshly cut," Bert remarked. "Someone must have been here recently and cut down the tree and all the brush on this side."

Charlie looked dismayed. "That spoils everything. Now we can't use the oak for the center of our maze."

"Sure we can," said Bert. "Let's pull up a lot of bushes and bring them here. Then we'll dig rows of holes and plant the bushes in them to make paths."

"Good idea," Nan agreed. "Then this part of the maze won't look any different from the rest."

"Swell," said Charlie. "Let's get the cord and the stakes."

"We'll be back in a second," Bert told his twin. He and Charlie made their way through the miniature jungle and across the clearing to the camp.

"Where's my duffle bag, Sam?" Bert asked the smiling man. "It has steel tape and cord in it. I want to lay out the maze."

Sam pointed to one of the pup tents. "Your bag's in there," he said. "And the bundle of stakes is in there too. I'll help you all tomorrow, but now I'm going to catch some fish for our supper."

"I hope you get a whopper," Bert told him. "I'm hungry as a wolf."

He dragged out the duffle bag and found the cord and measuring tape. Charlie picked up the bundle of stakes, and the boys ran back toward the woods. The younger twins hurried after them to offer their assistance.

"You two had better stay out of the woods until we get some paths cleared," Bert told them.

"All right. We'll play hide and seek around the trees at the edge of the woods," Freddie said.

When Bert and Charlie rejoined Nan, she said, "I want to show you something." She led them to the north end of the open section. Here was a clump of thick bushes extending left and right of an opening about two feet wide. "Wouldn't this be good for the entrance to the maze?" she asked.

"Perfect, if it's the right distance to the oak tree," Bert declared. "Let's measure." He took the steel tape from his pocket. "Charlie, take this, will you, and walk toward the oak as far as the tape will stretch."

Charlie did as Bert asked. "This is six feet," he announced. "The end of the line."

"Now Nan, will you stand in that place?" Bert asked. "And Charlie, go another six feet, please."

When this was done Bert asked Charlie to do it all over again. "The maze should measure twenty-four feet on the north side," he said. "The south end will be a little shorter than that."

Charlie went on. Finally he called, grinning, "It's exactly twenty-four feet to the tree!"

"Swell." Bert drove in a stake.

The three children now measured off twenty-four feet from east to west and drove in more stakes.

"Now we'll mark out the paths in this cleared part," Bert said. "They turn and twist so much I'll have to lay the cord in a—"

A loud scream interrupted him.

"That's Flossie!" cried Nan, as she started to scramble back through the thicket.

Bert and Charlie followed and soon came to where Flossie stood staring at the woods which bordered the clearing at that point.

"A boy was peeking at me!" she cried. "He

"Six feet," Charlie announced. "The end of the line."

was in those bushes. His face was all blue. Oo, maybe he was Danny Rugg."

At the mention of Danny's name, Bert went crashing into the shrubs which were very dense. As he broke through, he caught a glimpse of a boy darting away among the trees.

"If Danny Rugg's on this island we're in for trouble," Bert told the others in disgust. "How would he ever get here anyway?"

"I guess Danny could get to the moon if he wanted to," a small voice piped up as Freddie crawled out from behind a big log near by.

"Freddie Bobbsey! Is that where you were hiding?" cried his twin. "No wonder I couldn't find you!"

"I got stuck on a nail or something," Freddie replied. "Look, Nan, I tore my pants."

"My goodness! You certainly did, Freddie!" Nan went to see what had made the long tear in his clothes. "Bert," she called, "this log is hollow, and there's a nail sticking out of it."

Mr. and Mrs. Bobbsey came at that moment to see how the maze was progressing. Mr. Bobbsey looked at the log. "This has been hollowed out and put to some use," he remarked. "Something was nailed inside but has rotted away and left the nail. I wonder what it was used for."

"It's a mystery," Bert said as he led his father through the underbrush to where the children had started to lay out cord to indicate the paths.

"We are making the paths sixteen inches across," Bert explained. "The hedges between them will be about eighteen inches wide and five and a half feet high."

"You've certainly made a good start," his father said.

He and Mrs. Bobbsey and the younger twins returned to the camp with Snap. The two boys and Nan kept on working until a blast from Sam's bugle summoned them to supper.

"Well, we really have something to show for our work," Charlie remarked as he looked at the well-placed stakes and curving, cord-marked paths. "The maze is beginning to take shape."

Their supper tasted delicious out in the fresh, balmy air where they could hear the water lapping at the shore below.

"Sam, this fish is the best ever!" said Bert, as Sam, who was passing it, came to offer the boy a second helping.

Sam grinned, for he had not only caught the fish, but had grilled it also. "Bass is good eating," he said modestly. "And I guess you all are real hungry."

Later, when the first star appeared, Flossie cried, "I'm going to wish on it! Don't anybody ask me what I wished."

"We won't," said Bert. "I'm going to get my

sleeping bag. Boy! Will that feel good tonight!"

"And how!" Charlie agreed. "I'll get mine too."

"I didn't just wish that we'd have pancakes tomorrow," Flossie said as she gazed at the first star. "There's something else too."

"You wished for real maple syrup," guessed her twin, giggling.

"Freddie Bobbsey! That's not fair!" cried Flossie. "How did you know?"

"Your wish will come true if you go to bed now, little sweet fairy," Mrs. Bobbsey said, laughing.

Snap came running from the service tent as Bert and Charlie spread their sleeping bags out under the stars. He curled up between them happily.

Bert patted the dog's smooth white head. "You'll be taking half my bed before morning, you old rascal," he said, chuckling. Then he saw that Charlie was already asleep so he kept quiet. More stars came out but Bert's eyes refused to stay open very long to watch the twinkling display.

Some time in the night he awoke suddenly. There had been a thud, as though someone or something had fallen heavily. Snap had heard the noise too, and was on his feet instantly, ears alert, looking toward the woods. In a moment he bounded away. The night was so dark, despite the stars, that the white blur of Snap's coat was soon lost to sight. He returned presently, however, and lay down.

"Everything all right, old fellow?" Bert asked.

Snap wagged his tail. Then he and Bert both went back to sleep.

Bert awoke early. Remembering the thud, he dashed off with Snap across the clearing. He went through the thicket to the north side of the oak and then stopped astounded.

All the cord, which the children has so carefully tied to the stakes, lay in a tangled heap, and most of the stakes had disappeared!

CHAPTER VIII

FREDDIE'S STRANGE FIRE

"NAN! Charlie!" shouted Bert as he ran back to camp. "Someone has wrecked our maze!"

Charlie hurried to zip out of his sleeping bag. Everyone else ran from their tents.

"What did you say, Bert?" Nan asked, astonished.

"The cords are all broken, and half the stakes are gone!" Bert panted. "No wonder Snap barked and ran over there last night."

"Where's Snap now?" Mr. Bobbsey asked.

"I guess he stayed to look around," Bert said. "Snap went over with me just now."

"Why would anyone want to spoil your labo—labo—your *maze?*" Freddie spoke up.

"It was that mean old Danny Rugg!" declared Flossie. "He's got a blue face now just to scare people."

"It's a good thing we have more cord," Charlie said. "We can fix the paths again this morning."

"We'll all help," Nan said, "but how do we know they won't be wrecked again tonight?"

Sam grinned. "I just think that old Snap and I will sleep over there tonight," he said.

"We have an extra sleeping bag, Sam," Mr. Bobbsey remarked. "If you really want to act as guard, take your bugle so you can call if you need me."

"Fine, Mr. Bobbsey," said Sam, "and right now I think I'll go do a little inspectin' myself and fetch Snap."

He strolled off. In a few minutes, Mrs. Bobbsey called, "Breakfast is ready." She showed her family a griddle full of crisp, golden pancakes. "Line up with your plates."

The others hurried to obey, and soon they were seated in a circle on the ground.

"Yum!" exclaimed Flossie as she poured rich maple syrup over her cakes. "Both my star wishes came true."

As everyone ate, Bert said, "Dad, do you think the person who wrecked things might have been Pen Whiteside? I believe he thinks we have the money with us."

"That hardly seems possible," his father answered. "And if it were, I can't see why he'd be anywhere near your labyrinth. He'd come by boat or through the woods."

"Here comes Snap!" cried Flossie. "He has something in his mouth."

The white dog was bounding across the clearing toward them, playfully shaking the object which he carried.

"It's a bird!" cried Nan. "Oh, I hope it's not dead."

"Snap never catches birds," said Bert. "It's a dead mole or a mouse, more likely."

Nan ran toward Snap, who dodged around her playfully. He did not realize, though, that Bert was near by. Bert grabbed him.

"I've got you. Drop it, boy! Oh, look," he exclaimed, "Snap's found the first clue. Whoever visited us last night lost a toupee!" Bert held up a false hairpiece by two fingers.

"Wowee!" exclaimed Freddie, and Mr. Bobbsey said, "The owner is probably an old or a middle-aged man. Did Pen Whiteside wear a toupee?"

"We couldn't see him plainly enough to be sure," Nan remarked. "But, as I remember, his hair *was* that same shade of mousy brown."

"Well, anyway, it couldn't have been Danny Rugg," Flossie piped up. "Daddy, why do men wear wigs?"

"Sometimes men like to wear toupees when they are almost bald, my sweet fairy," he told her.

"I guess Snap scared him away before he had time to hunt for it." Bert laughed.

"We'll have to cut a lot more stakes before we can lay out those paths again," Charlie reminded Bert as they finished breakfast.

Sam, who had just returned, overheard him. "Look over there by the kitchen tent, Bert." He pointed to a fine pile of new stakes, which the boys had not noticed.

"Sam! Did you make these?" Bert asked in surprise.

The kindly man grinned. "I wasn't sleepy last night, so I whittled those out," he said. "I guess you can use 'em."

"I'll say we can!" cried Bert. "Now we can get right to work marking off the paths."

"I'll come over to help you cut some brush in a little while," Sam said. "We'll soon get that part of the maze into shape."

"Did you find any more clues to the toupee man?" Bert asked him.

"No, I didn't, Bert. I guess he's a slick kind of fellow."

Bert ran to join Charlie and Mr. Bobbsey, who were walking toward the labyrinth.

"I'll bring you more cord later today, Bert," Mr. Bobbsey told his son. "I have to go over to Lakeport for a while this morning."

"Thanks, Dad," Bert said. "In the meantime, we may be able to untangle some of the old cord."

"I'm glad you're not discouraged," Mr. Bobbsey said. "I can't understand who would deliberately want to wreck your work."

Nan, who had come on ahead to the labyrinth, was bending over and lifting the mass of cords. "I think I can untangle these alone," she announced. "But it will take time— Ooh! What's this?" Something shiny had fallen out of the knotted strands which she held.

"It's a ring!" cried Charlie. "A diamond ring!" He picked up the ring and handed it to Mr. Bobbsey.

"If I'm any judge of stones, this is a very fine diamond," the twins' father said, after examining the gem.

"Wow!" exclaimed Bert. "What'll we do with it?"

"I'd better take this and the toupee to the Lakeport police," his father said. "The ring may have been lost or stolen. At any rate, we don't want to keep it here."

As he started back to the clearing to take the launch, he met Mrs. Bobbsey and the younger twins.

"Mother says we may go with you, Daddy," Freddie said. "I want to get my pumper."

Flossie grabbed her father's hand. "I'd love to get my new doll, Linda."

"Very well," Mr. Bobbsey said, smiling. "I'll be glad to have your company. Let's go!"

They met Sam coming to cut brush, armed with all his implements.

"You look like a real woodcutter, Sam," Mr. Bobbsey remarked.

"Yes, sir," Sam replied, grinning. "We're going to cut paths right through that jungle, one, two, three."

Mr. Bobbsey and the younger twins said good-by and started off aboard the *Tall Timber.* In a little while they were approaching the dock at the lumberyard. Suddenly a boat passed them, going at full speed.

Freddie looked after it. "That's the one we saw yesterday. Remember? The boat with the noisy outboard motor?"

"Um, I remember," said Flossie. "He slapped the *Tall Timber* hard with his old waves."

After Mr. Bobbsey had docked, he went for the station wagon and they rode to the police station to leave the ring and the toupee. Chief Malone was amazed at the story.

"I'll let you know if anyone reports the loss," he promised. "By the way, no one has claimed that four hundred and ninety dollars yet."

The Bobbseys now went to their own home. Dinah was sweeping the front porch. She uttered a whoop of joy when she saw the twins.

"I'm sure glad to see your little faces again," she cried. "Seems like you been gone a month."

Snoop came purring and rubbing against their legs, telling in his own way how much he, too, had missed his playmates.

"I'll be back at two o'clock to get the children," Mr. Bobbsey told Dinah as he left for the office.

Freddie ran upstairs to get his fire engine pumper and put it by the front door. He was determined not to forget it again.

"I'll make a splendiferous cake for you to take back with you," Dinah told the twins.

"Coconut?" cried Freddie.

"Chocolate?" Flossie insisted.

"We'll have a little of each," the easygoing cook decided. "A chocolate cake with coconut icing."

She went into the kitchen to make it, while the twins played outdoors. Before two, Mr. Bobbsey telephoned, asking Dinah to bring Freddie and Flossie to the dock at the lumberyard, as he was too busy to leave the office.

Freddie led the way down the front walk with his pumper in tow. Flossie came next, carrying Linda. Dinah brought up the rear, bearing the cake in a large box. They walked slowly along the pleasant streets to the lumberyard dock. As they neared the boathouse, the twins saw a puff of smoke curl out of its open window.

"Fire!" shouted Freddie, and began to run. "It's a good thing I have my pumper!"

Flossie raced after him and Dinah tried to hurry too. But this was hard since she was heavy-set and the cake was awkward to carry.

Freddie flung open the side door of the boat-

house and directed a stream of water from his pumper full force into the building. Suddenly a man darted out, nearly knocking the little fire-man into the water. In the man's hand was a wet cigar.

"Get out of the way!" he snapped, as he tried to dodge the stream of water. Freddie had dropped the pumper in his surprise, but the water continued to soak the legs of the man's blue trousers.

He ran with a decided limp around the corner of the boathouse and disappeared behind a pile of lumber. Dinah and the twins noticed that he had red hair and a red mustache, but his hat was pulled down so far over his eyes that they scarcely saw his features at all.

Dinah doubled up with laughter, and nearly dropped the cake. "Ha, ha, ho, ho," she gurgled. "Freddie, you were only putting out the fire in the gentleman's cigar!"

The young fireman had to laugh too, but he was a little curious. "What was that man doing in our boathouse?" he asked.

Flossie stopped giggling long enough to say, "I don't know. But he did look funny—all wet."

Mr. Bobbsey came up as they were still laughing. When they told him the story, he chuckled too. "But we'll have to keep the boathouse locked from now on," he said.

He stepped to a phone inside the building and told one of the workmen to do this. Then he and the twins said good-by to Dinah. They promised to take good care of the cake. Mr. Bobbsey carried it carefully onto the launch and placed it on the counter in the cabin.

Freddie, meanwhile, was busy getting his pumper in shape to bring aboard, when Flossie stooped to pick up something from the floor of the boathouse. It was a man's green bow necktie.

"Well," said Mr. Bobbsey, when she showed it to him, "we're getting a mysterious collection of articles. I wonder if that red-haired man dropped this."

"Prob'ly," said Flossie. "But I don't think it's pretty."

Freddie was thoughtful. "Daddy," he finally said, "the man who took the lady's purse—Mrs. Hart—he had red hair."

"But did he have a mustache?" Mr. Bobbsey asked.

"I guess he didn't," Freddie decided. "So the man in the boathouse wasn't bad after all."

He climbed aboard the *Tall Timber* with Flossie and his father, and they set off for the camp on Blueberry Island. During supper that evening, the small twins made everyone laugh as they told about Freddie and the boathouse "fire." Then, after they finished eating Dinah's delicious cake, Flossie showed the green bow tie to the family.

"Say!" Bert exclaimed. "I've seen that tie before—or else its twin."

"I know," Nan spoke up quickly. "Pen Whiteside had one on. I remember thinking what an ugly color it was."

"But that wasn't Mr. Whiteside who came out of the boathouse," declared Freddie. "This man was lame and had red hair and a big red mustache."

"Well, we'll put this necktie away to show the police later," said Mr. Bobbsey. "And, by the way, I called them today before I left the office. They've still had no report of a diamond ring or a toupee being lost or stolen. They think maybe some picnicker lost them."

Nan and Bert looked at each other. They felt sure there was more to the mystery than this. What about the boy who had peered at them through the bushes?

When bedtime came, Bert said, "It's a super-duper night! Look at all those stars. Dad, may Charlie and I take our sleeping bags and sleep on the deck of the boat?"

"Are the stars any brighter over the water?" his father teased. "Well, I guess it will be okay. Sam can row you out. Sound the horn when you want to come back in the morning."

The boys hurried to get their sleeping bags, then went with Sam to the rowboat. They pushed it off shore, climbed in, and headed for the *Tall Timber*.

"If you want me in the night for anything, all you have to do is blow that horn," Sam told Bert and Charlie.

They reached the launch in another minute, and the boys said good night to Sam.

"Have a good sleep, boys," the man called with a smile as the boys climbed onto the deck of the *Tall Timber.*

Bert and Charlie crawled into their sleeping bags and lay down. The stars *did* seem brighter over the water, and the boys watched them as they talked. Then as they grew sleepy, the two became quiet.

Bert was not quite asleep when he heard something scrape softly against the side of the boat. He listened intently. Then Charlie touched his hand in the dark. "There's a boat alongside," he whispered. "I heard oars."

CHAPTER IX

A BAD TUMBLE

AS BERT and Charlie listened, their hearts pounded. They could hear the unmistakable drag of oars being pulled into a boat.

The boys got out of their sleeping bags in a hurry and looked over the rail. A small rowboat was drawn up beside the *Tall Timber,* and a man was tying it to the stern rail of the larger boat.

"Dad, is that you?" Bert called loudly.

Instantly, the man ducked his head and ripped the rowboat free, breaking the cord. He muttered something about a "mistake," as he hurried the oars back into their locks. In a moment he rowed off and was soon lost in the darkness of the shoreline.

"Well!" said Charlie. "What do you make of that?"

"I wonder who it was and what he wanted," Bert said. "Did you get a good look at him?"

"No." Charlie stared into the darkness. "Do you suppose that was Pen Whiteside and he thinks we have the money on board?"

Bert thought this over. "My guess is that someone saw the *Tall Timber* in this inlet and thought he might find something worth stealing on board. I wonder who lives on the nearest small island."

"There are about six of them not far away from Blueberry," Charlie remarked. "Anyway I think we scared the fellow. He won't be back tonight."

"Righto!" Bert replied. "I guess we needn't toot the boat's horn for help."

When Bert awoke in the morning Charlie was already up, with his sleeping bag rolled into a neat bundle. "Hi!" he said.

Bert scrambled to his feet and looked over the rail of the boat. "Did I dream that we had a visitor last night?" he asked, rubbing his eyes.

"I had the same dream, if it was one," Charlie declared.

Bert suddenly remembered something. He ran to the stern rail. Sure enough! There was a piece of broken cord tied there. "Hot diggity!" he exclaimed as he untied it. "This might be a clue, Charlie. Look at this cord!"

"That's some of the cord from the maze!"

Charlie yelled. "Or some just like it. Well, what do you know!"

"I know it's time for breakfast," Bert said, looking at his watch. "Let's swim ashore and not wait to call Sam to come with the boat."

"Righto!" agreed Charlie.

Both boys were wearing cotton shorts and sweat shirts. They put their sleeping bags into the cabin and then dived into the water.

"I'll race you," Charlie called, as they set out for the beach.

The two boys arrived on the strip of sand almost at the same moment. Sam was just coming out of the woodland path.

"Good morning," he said. "I was just on my way to fetch you."

"Did the labyrinth have any callers last night, Sam?" asked Bert, as he and Charlie walked back to camp with him.

"Not as I could see," Sam replied. "But Snap, he growled once something fierce and went sniffing all around. Then he came back and lay down again. The maze looked all right to me this morning."

The boys told Sam about their own caller.

"I reckon I'd better sleep on the launch with you tonight," he told them. "I'll take that big lantern that has the strong batteries. We'll flash it right in that fellow's face if he comes again."

"Good idea," Bert said as he and Charlie ran

toward the pup tents to change into dry clothes.

At breakfast they related the story to the family. Mrs. Bobbsey was disturbed. "Don't sleep there again without your father or Sam along," she said.

Mr. Bobbsey was interested in the piece of cord. "I think you're right, boys, in your suspicion about this. The man who wrecked your labyrinth is probably the same one who visited the *Tall Timber* last night."

"But why?" Nan asked. "What is he trying to do?"

This was a question no one could answer at the moment.

"Anyhow," said Mr. Bobbsey, "we mustn't let all this spoil our camping trip or the making of the maze!"

"No," said Nan. "After all, this is a test maze for the one Bert's going to build for the school fair."

Her father nodded, then said to Mrs. Bobbsey, "Mary, let's you and I take over the fishing today so Sam can help with the maze."

"That's a good idea," Mrs. Bobbsey agreed.

"Swell, Dad." Bert grinned. "We can use everybody over at the labyrinth this morning. Are we ready, kids?"

There was a chorus of "Yes," "Let's go," and "Ready, skipper!" The children ran across the clearing and pushed through the bushes to the oak tree. Sam followed, bringing his keen-edged machete and his saber saw.

"You give out the jobs, Bert," his twin suggested.

"All right," Bert agreed. "Charlie and I will stake out the paths again on the north side, and Nan can run the cord along them. We'll tell Sam which bushes to dig up for the hedges on each side of the paths."

"Okay, boss," Sam said, grinning. "Just give me the word." Bert went on, "Freddie and Flossie can clean the paths by gathering up the leaves and dried twigs."

Work started with great speed. Presently Bert said, "I'm going to take a look at the entrance." He ran over to it.

The others suddenly heard a crashing thud, and turned to see Bert lying flat on the ground. They hurried over to see what had happened. Bert sat up and stared at a cord stretched tightly between the bushes at each side of the entrance.

"I tripped over that cord," he explained. "Who put it here? It wasn't here yesterday. Wow! My ankle hurts!"

All denied any knowledge of the string. There were a number of suspects: the blue-faced boy, the man in the rowboat, or even Pen Whiteside.

Sam and Charlie helped Bert across the open ground to a grassy knoll on the bank of the lake. The bank was high above the water and filled with a rank growth of tall weeds and shrubbery.

"Now you sit here and rest your foot," Sam told Bert. "Charlie and I will do our best."

"I'll stay with you, Bert," Flossie said as she threw herself down on the knoll. "How nice the water sounds here! It goes in little slaps, doesn't it?" she remarked. "And then it swishes."

"Yes, it sounds mighty good," Bert agreed.

"I wonder how far down the water is," Flossie said, jumping up to look over the shrubbery.

"Don't lean on those bushes!" Bert warned her. "Look out!" He made a dive to catch Flossie as the bushes bent forward. She plunged head first, but he caught both of her feet in his hands.

"Help!" he shouted loudly, when he felt himself slipping too.

Sam and Charlie ran up swiftly to help pull the two back.

"Ooooh!" Flossie exclaimed, pushing the blond curls out of her eyes. "I almost fell into the boat down there."

"Boat? What boat?" Bert asked in amazement.

"There was a boat with a man in it right under here," Flossie said, pointing.

Charlie rushed to the edge. He pushed aside the bushes and looked down. "I don't see any boat," he said. Then he scanned the lake shore in both directions. "There's none in sight as far as I can see, Flossie."

He made a dive to catch Flossie

"It couldn't go away so fast!" exclaimed the bewildered little girl. "Look again, Charlie."

Sam and Nan looked too, but could see no boat along the coast of Blueberry Island. "Perhaps it was a log," Nan suggested to her sister.

"Nan Bobbsey! I know the difference between a boat with a man in it and a log!" Flossie cried, offended.

"But you had such a little glimpse, honey," Nan explained. "You hardly had time to see it."

"Besides, you were upside down," Freddie reminded her. "Things look awful funny that way."

"That's why I couldn't see the man's face very well," his twin said. "But he had a cap on his head, and he looked awf'ly big."

Flossie could not be shaken from her story, and finally the others gave up.

"Well, we'd better get back to work," Charlie said to Sam. "I was just measuring off one of the blind alleys near the oak."

They went across to the maze. Sam began to dig up bushes to use as hedges. Bert was eager to resume his part in the project, but the others insisted he stay off his sore ankle.

In a little while, Freddie's sharp ears caught the sound of his parents' voices. "Mommy and Daddy are back!" he cried. "Let's see if they caught some fish!" He and Flossie started off at full speed.

Nan, meanwhile, had sat down beside Bert. "Do you think Flossie really did see a boat?" she asked.

"Maybe," he answered. "I remember now that the water sounded as if it were lapping against something solid, like a boat."

"But how could it have disappeared so soon?" Nan asked, wide-eyed.

"It could have gone into one of the little coves."

Mr. and Mrs. Bobbsey came hurrying across the clearing to the knoll. When they heard what had happened to Bert, his father said, "Let me have a look at that ankle, Bert."

Bert removed his hiking shoe, and Mr. Bobbsey examined the ankle. Then he turned it gently and pressed slightly on the tender spots.

"I'm sure it's just a slight strain, son," he said. "Favor it for a day or two but walk on it some every day so it won't get stiff. It'll be all right before you know it."

"Thanks, Dad," Bert answered, greatly relieved. "It feels better already."

"Did you catch any fish?" asked Nan, smiling up at her pretty, sun-tanned mother.

"Indeed we did!" exclaimed Mrs. Bobbsey. "The bass were fairly jumping up to catch the hook. Can you children spare Sam to fix the fish for lunch? He does it much better than anyone else."

"Of course, Mother," Bert replied.

"I can measure," Nan offered, rising. "And Charlie can do some cutting with the clippers." She went across to the maze and spoke to Sam.

He grinned. "I'll go right away and tend to those fish." He went back to camp with Mr. and Mrs. Bobbsey.

Bert hobbled over to watch Nan and Charlie. Presently a slight movement in the underbrush at the edge of the woods caught his attention. He watched it, waiting. Then the bushes parted and he saw the head of a boy between the green leaves. The lad stared at the two children working on the maze.

"The boy with the blue face!" Bert thought excitedly. "Hello, there!" he called.

At his words the head disappeared.

CHAPTER X

A BLUEBERRY MISHAP

AS BERT said hello, Nan and Charlie looked up. Seeing no one else around, Nan, puzzled, asked, "Whom were you talking to, Bert?"

"The boy we thought was Danny Rugg. I guess I scared him away."

Suddenly the woodsy shrubbery swayed, and the strange boy stepped out before the startled children. He was about Bert's size and coloring, but the lower half of his face was stained blue.

"My name is Tommy Turner," he said shyly.

The campers were surprised. "Are you one of the Turners from the other end of the island?" Nan asked him.

"Yes, I am. And I didn't mean to spy on you. I was only trying to figure out what you all were doing over there by the tree."

Bert laughed. "I don't blame you for wondering, Tommy," he said, "but why did you run away the other day? We thought you were a boy we know named Danny Rugg, who's always making trouble."

"I guess I was ashamed to be caught peeking," Tommy replied, blushing.

Freddie and Flossie ran up just then, and Nan introduced them to Tommy. She told the small twins he was the one they had mistaken for Danny.

"Well, I'm glad it's you and not Danny," Freddie told him. "We know you, Tommy. I mean, we know your mother and she told us about you."

"She told me about all of you, too," the boy said, smiling in a friendly way.

Flossie had been staring at Tommy intently. "Have you been picking blueberries and eating them?" she asked him.

"Yes, I guess my face is all stained." Tommy tried to wipe it with the ragged sleeve of his shirt. "Sometimes I get so hungry that I have to eat a few. I don't take very many, though, because I want to sell as many quarts as I can."

"Are you hungry now, Tommy?" Freddie asked. "I am, and lunch is 'most ready. You stay and have some."

The blueberry boy's eyes brightened. Then he said, "Oh no, thank you, I couldn't do that. I have to pick more berries because the man from the store on Rand Island is coming to get them this evening."

"Freddie and I will help you pick more after lunch," Flossie offered eagerly. "Do stay!"

"Yes, Tommy," Nan urged. "Two helpers will get you as many berries as you could pick by yourself during lunchtime."

"All right then." Tommy grinned. "I'll get my bucket." He disappeared behind the bushes and returned with a pail half full of fine blueberries.

"There must be quarts and quarts there!" Nan exclaimed. "I never saw so many at once."

Tommy smiled. "That's about three quarts. I picked them in an hour this morning. This is a good blueberry year. Sometimes I don't get more'n ten quarts all season."

"Would you like to see our labyrinth, Tommy?" Charlie asked, as Tommy's eyes turned to the staked-out paths and the transplanted hedges.

"Your what?" he asked with a puzzled glance at Charlie.

"It's a maze," explained Freddie. "It's like a puzzle, only it's a garden."

Tommy grinned. "It sure looks like a puzzle," he remarked.

Charlie showed Tommy the design of the maze which Bert had drawn. The blueberry boy had been carrying his pail of berries. Now he set it on the ground in the shade while he stared at the paper.

"A person sure could get all mixed up in this maze," he remarked. "It's super."

Charlie told him about the school fair and why he and Bert were making the trial labyrinth. "Maybe you can come to the fair," he invited.

"I hope I can be there," said Tommy. "I'll sure try."

As they left the maze he remembered his pail and turned to get it. At that minute Freddie came running to announce, "We're having a picnic on the beach! Hurry, so we can go in swimming first."

"Why don't you leave your pail where it is?" Charlie suggested to Tommy. "It will be all right there."

"Okay," the boy agreed, and they ran to join Nan and Bert, who were walking on ahead.

"Tommy, I'll lend you a pair of my swimming trunks," Bert offered.

"That would be swell, Bert. I'm pretty big for ten years old, I guess," Tommy replied, as they went to the pup tent to change.

The children had their dip, then ate lunch on the warm sand. Mr. and Mrs. Bobbsey made Tommy very welcome, and the time passed quickly.

After a happy hour Tommy rose and said to Mrs. Bobbsey, "Thank you. That was an awfully good lunch. Now I must get back to my job."

"Flossie and I are going to help Tommy pick berries this afternoon," Freddie told his mother.

"All right, dear, but don't go too far into the woods," Mrs. Bobbsey said.

"There's a fine stand of blueberries just back of the clearing," Tommy told her. "We won't have to go far."

"I saw a couple of small baskets in the big tent," Sam told Freddie and Flossie. "I'll get them for you all." He ran up to the camp ahead of the twins with Charlie and Tommy close behind.

When they reached the tent, Charlie said, "I'll go get your pail for you, Tommy." He went ahead while Tommy waited for the twins. They soon arrived.

"These are nice big baskets," Flossie commented, as Sam handed her one and she swung it over her arm. "I can get lots of berries in here," she added, as they all started toward the woods.

In a few moments they met Charlie coming from among the bushes. "Did you put your pail some other place, Tommy?" he asked. "It's not where I thought you left it."

"No," replied the boy. "It must be in there on the ground. I'll go back with you and look."

They hurried behind the tall shrubbery, but

soon returned. "The pail has disappeared!" Charlie said, bewildered. "We've looked everywhere."

"Golly, I can't lose that bucket!" Tommy said. "And all those berries, too!"

Nan and Bert went to search but were no more successful than Charlie. Then Sam tried, but did not find it.

"Where *could* the pail have gone?" Tommy asked, bewildered.

"Maybe a bear took it," Flossie suggested.

"There are no bears on the island," said Tommy. "A deer might eat the berries, but he wouldn't carry away the pail. Some person took it."

"I'm terribly sorry, Tommy!" said Nan. She was wondering if the strange man in the rowboat Bert and Charlie had seen might have been responsible.

"I'll get you another pail," Flossie offered, running off toward camp.

Soon she came hurrying back with a bright new pail and handed it to Tommy. "We'll lend you this one," she said, smiling.

Tommy thanked her. Then he and the little twins went into the woods. He led the way among the trees and heavy underbrush while Flossie and Freddie followed. Tommy held back low-lying branches which would have been hard for the smaller children to push aside.

"There aren't many paths in these woods, are there?" Freddie observed, after he had tripped on a tough creeper.

"There are only three," Tommy told him. "One is the trail we took from your camp to the beach. Another runs from the clearing by my home to the cabin with the boathouse where you went that day."

"Oh, you mean the Whitesides' cabin?" Flossie spoke up. "There's a mother and her son Pen."

"I see," said Tommy. "The third path on the island," he went on, "runs from the Whitesides' cabin through the woods up to the big oak tree."

"Do you mean Bert's oak tree—the one in the maze?" queried Freddie.

"Yes."

"It's a funny house where the Whitesides live," said Freddie. "They even have bats in it."

Flossie was puffing along behind them. Tommy stopped. "See those bushes ahead with the shiny green leaves?" he asked. "Those are the blueberries."

He stepped over to the beautiful green shrubs and began dropping the delicious berries into his pail. The twins felt proud as their own baskets filled rapidly.

"I wish I could pick with two hands at once!" Freddie exclaimed. "There's too many for just one hand."

Tommy laughed. "Don't you wish sometimes that you were an octopus with eight arms and a hand at the end of each one?"

Freddie grinned, thinking how funny an octopus would look picking blueberries.

"How could an octopus stand up?" asked Flossie. She was trying to remember whether it had feet or not.

"I guess," replied Tommy, "that it would have to spread itself over the bush. It doesn't have anything like feet to stand on."

Freddie said he was going around to the other side of the patch of bushes to do more picking. A moment later he called, "I'm going to play octopus."

He threw himself sprawling over the fruit-laden bush. Before Flossie and Tommy knew what was happening, Freddie came crashing down upon them and landed head first in Tommy's brimming bucket of blueberries!

"Freddie Bobbsey!" cried Flossie. "You've ruined Tommy's nice berries!"

Tommy was laughing so hard that he could scarcely pull the little boy up to his feet. "That's all right," he said. "There are lots more here."

Freddie wiped his sticky, dripping, bluish-red face with his sleeve. Streaks of blue juice ran down from his hair across his round cheeks.

"You'll have to go swimming again," said Flossie. "With a cake of soap. We'd better go."

Tommy dumped out the crushed blueberries, then the twins put their good ones into his big pail. The island boy thanked them again for lunch and the swim, then said good-by.

"I'll come again soon," he promised, "And return your mother's pail."

"And we'll keep looking for yours," Freddie promised.

The twins hurried off. When they arrived in camp, Mrs. Bobbsey gasped. "Why, Freddie! What happened?"

"I took a blueberry bath," he said, grinning. "But now I'll take a white shampoo."

That evening, a few hours after supper, Bert and Charlie said they were ready to go to the *Tall Timber*. Sam went with the boys, and Mr. Bobbsey rowed them out to the launch.

"I hope nothing disturbs you," he said when he was ready to leave.

"We'll be on the look-out just in case," Bert declared. "Good night, Dad."

Sam and the boys had the camp's powerful lantern with them, ready to be turned on at the first sign of trouble. The three watched for the mysterious caller of the previous night until twelve o'clock. Then, unable to stay awake any longer, they gave up their vigil and settled down to sleep.

It was a few minutes later that Bert heard the stealthy sound of oars near by. He nudged Charlie, and they sat up. Sam too had awakened and was holding the lantern in position, ready to press the button.

They all crept to the rail and listened. There was a rowboat alongside the launch. Sam pressed the button of the lantern. A great beam of light fell full upon the rowboat below.

For a fraction of a second the man in it stared

up at them. He had red hair and a mustache. Instantly he ducked his head and with a mighty pull on the oars sent his boat into the shadows along the shore.

"How'd he get out of this here light so fast?" asked the bewildered Sam. "He must be powerful strong on the oars."

"Remember how he broke that heavy cord last night with one jerk?" asked Bert. "He has the strength of a giant. Who *is* he, anyway?"

CHAPTER XI

THE *TALL TIMBER'S* SECRET

"WE'D BETTER sleep in shifts," Bert suggested.

"We sure had," Sam agreed. "If we all go to sleep, that fellow might try to slip on board. But s'pose I do the watchin'. You boys need your rest."

"Oh, no," Bert insisted. "In fact, I'd like to be the one to catch that snooper and find out what he wants."

It was arranged that each of them would stand watch for two hours. Sam took the first watch. As the two boys crawled into their sleeping bags, he settled himself in the stern with the flash lantern. "No one's goin' to sneak on this boat 'less I see him," he told himself.

When he woke Charlie later, Sam reported that there had been no disturbance.

"Maybe we scared off that man," Charlie said.

"But I'd like to know where he came from."

As Sam began to snore gently, Charlie stared off into the darkness. Suddenly the boy was startled by a splash in the water. He crept to the rail. There was another splash. "Oh, it's only a fish jumping out of the water," he muttered.

Finally at four o'clock he awakened Bert. "All I heard was a fish," he reported, stretching sleepily.

Soon after six o'clock Sam and Charlie awoke. The boys offered to swim ashore and bring the rowboat out to get Sam. He nodded and waited at the rail, watching them.

"They sure are good swimmers," he thought.

Charlie insisted that Bert go ahead to camp and put on dry clothes, while he went out for Sam. "You have to take it easy with that bad ankle, you know," he said.

At breakfast the other Bobbseys listened in amazement to the story of the night's adventures. They were particularly interested in Bert's description of the man in the rowboat.

Flossie jumped up excitedly. "That's the one Freddie sprayed his pumper on in the boathouse," she cried. "He had red hair and a mustache, too. I guess he's coming to get the green necktie he lost."

"I doubt that," said Mr. Bobbsey.

"Do you suppose," asked Nan, "that he wants to steal the *Tall Timber?*"

"Oh, how awful!" Flossie exclaimed.

Mrs. Bobbsey suggested that the twins stop worrying about this and enjoy their breakfast. "And tonight let's build a bonfire and have a marshmallow roast," she suggested.

"Goody!" exclaimed Freddie and Flossie.

After breakfast Mr. Bobbsey said he was taking the launch over to Rand Island. "I'm going to the little store there for a newspaper and a few supplies," he explained.

"May we go with you, Daddy?" asked Freddie. "I'd like to see how Tommy's blueberries are selling."

Mr. Bobbsey laughed. "You think maybe you picked too many? Yes, you may go. I'll call you when I'm ready."

Freddie and Flossie ran to catch up with the older children, who were already heading for the maze. Reaching the oak tree, they broke into pleased grins at their work. The north end was finished and looked very fine, they thought, with its tall green hedges and series of paths.

"Today we'll lay out the south end," Bert announced.

Sam gazed at the thicket, holding his fine machete and saber saw. "The finished part is so twisted I get all kind o' flustered when I try to walk in it," he said, chuckling. "And now we're goin' to make another. Oh my! Where do you want me to cut next, Bert?"

"I'll show you," Bert replied. "But first I'll lay the cord on top of the bushes to mark the paths. Then you can cut between the strings."

Bert stepped back quickly to start, but his weak ankle turned and he felt a stab of pain. He winced and nearly fell. "I'll be okay in a minute," he insisted.

"You'd better sit down a while, Bert, and rest your ankle," Nan suggested. "Charlie and I can lay out the string for the paths. You're apt to turn your ankle again in this thicket."

Mr. Bobbsey, who had come to get Flossie and Freddie, overheard the remark. "Why don't you come with us, Bert?" he said. "You can rest your foot on the boat."

"All right, Dad. I think I will." Bert got to his feet and limped after his father and the small twins to the beach. He felt very much out of sorts because he wanted to work on the maze himself. But aboard the launch, as it sped toward Rand Island, he felt better and enjoyed the ride.

Presently Flossie asked, "Aren't there any games on the boat, Daddy, that Freddie and I could play with?"

Mr. Bobbsey glanced around as he sat at the wheel. "If there are any, they'd be in a locker, sweet fairy."

Between them, Flossie and Freddie lifted one of the heavy seat-lockers in the cabin. Then they stood still, staring at what they saw inside.

"Daddy!" cried Freddie. "There's a man's clothes in here!"

"And his hair too," added Flossie. "Another brown wig!"

"And a sack full of lumpy things," said Freddie.

Bert was beside the twins in a second. As his father watched in astonishment, Bert unwound the cord which held the top of the sack.

"Wow!" exclaimed Freddie. "This bag is full of money and watches and stuff."

"It must be stolen property," said Mr. Bobbsey.

"Now we know what that red-haired fellow was after," Bert declared. "Say, I wonder if he's the one who put the stuff here in the first place."

"Sure he did," said Freddie. "The man at our boathouse that I pumped water on was hiding it in the *Tall Timber* right then."

Mr. Bobbsey smiled. "Perhaps. In any case, we'll have to take everything to the Lakeport police." He made a wide circle with the launch and headed for the lumberyard dock.

Bert, meanwhile, took an empty duffle bag out of the locker and put the brown wig, the clothes, and the sack in it. As the four Bobbseys walked into police headquarters some time later, the chief smiled at them from his high desk.

"No report on Aunt Emma's money yet," he said. "Nor on that toupee or the diamond ring."

"We have found something else, Chief," Bert remarked as he handed over the duffle bag and also showed the green tie.

Chief Malone gave a long whistle as he took the articles out of the bag and put them on his desk. There were watches, bracelets, rings, men's wallets, loose change, and many rolls of bills.

"Where did you find this?" he asked.

Bert told him and also told about the efforts of the man in the rowboat to board the launch.

"This is a very important discovery," the chief told the Bobbseys. "The wig and clothes show that the thieves are using disguises to fool the police. But now that we know it, our job of tracking them down will be easier."

Freddie told how he had turned the pumper on the red-haired man in the boathouse.

Chief Malone laughed. "You Bobbsey twins are certainly giving these thieves a bad time," he said. "Now I am going to call some of the people who have been robbed. They can claim their possessions, thanks to you."

As they left the police station, Bert said, "Dad, may I have the key to the boathouse while you do your errands? I'd like to look around and see if I can find out anything more."

His father drove him to the boathouse and gave Bert the keys. As the boy unlocked the door he heard a noisy outboard motorboat coming down the lake.

It was the one which had whizzed by a couple of days before, then stopped so suddenly and disappeared! As Bert watched intently, the motorboat did exactly the same thing again!

"I'd like to know what that pilot is up to," the boy thought.

As soon as Mr. Bobbsey and the small twins returned, he told them about the mysterious boat. "I'm sure it docked right near here," Bert said, "but Sam told me the other day there aren't any docks around except ours."

"There's an old loading wharf at the edge of the lumberyard," Mr. Bobbsey replied. "It was used years ago when the lumber company loaded large vessels direct from the tramway."

"What's a tramway?" Freddie asked.

"Tracks on which wagons run."

"Like a railroad?"

"Yes. But the old wharf is too high for passengers from a small boat to step onto."

"Let's run up that way as we leave," Bert suggested, "and take a look anyhow."

Mr. Bobbsey backed the *Tall Timber* and went along the shore slowly. "There's the old wharf," he said. "It's almost hidden by trees now."

The group peered into the darkness beneath the wharf, but could see nothing. Freddie opened a locker and took out the binoculars. These were always returned to the boat whenever anyone went out in the *Tall Timber*. He held them to his eyes.

"Oh, I see it—that man's boat!" Freddie exclaimed. "Away back underneath. Nobody's in it." He handed the binoculars to Bert. "You look."

Bert stared intently as the launch came to a halt. "Yes, that is the green boat with the outboard motor, and Freddie's right. Nobody's in it."

"Maybe the man's hiding on the floor," said Flossie. "Ooh, it's spooky here. Let's go!"

"All right, little sweet fairy," her father replied, and started the motor.

"Nobody's hiding. I can see every inch of the boat now," Bert told the others. "The man's gone."

"I guess we'd better head for camp," said his father as he swung the launch around in a wide circle. "The next time I go to town," he added, "I'll tell the police about this fellow and his free parking place!"

When they reached Blueberry Island, Flossie bubbled over with the whole story. The campers listened in amazement.

"So the clothes and the loot were what our visitor wanted!" exclaimed Charlie. "What a find!"

"If he comes again tonight," said Bert with a grin, "I'll tell him that he can find his clothes and stuff at the police station!"

That afternoon all the twins, with Charlie and Sam, worked hard on the maze. By evening every path in the south end had been cut.

"All this maze needs," Sam remarked, "is a little slickin' up, and she'll be the best one ever."

"I just love it," said Flossie, "but I wouldn't want to get lost in the maze."

Freddie chuckled. "If a big animal should get inside, he might not be able to get out. Then we'd have to rescue him."

"But not bears," declared Flossie firmly.

"Don't you remember, there aren't any bears on Blueberry Island," Nan reminded her sister.

Finally everyone gathered on the beach for supper. Dessert was marshmallows roasted on stout twigs over a bonfire.

"They're fabulous, Mother," said Nan, munching one which was toasted a golden brown.

"Yes," Freddie agreed. "But I can't cook 'em fast enough."

Nan laughed. "Put two on your stick at one time." Freddie tried this and found that it worked very well.

After supper the children played games for a while, then started for bed one by one. It was after ten before Sam and the two older boys went to the launch.

"I'll keep watch," Sam offered. "You get your sleep."

"No, we'll take turns, like last night," Bert declared.

It was so still and peaceful out on the lake that Sam, who took the first turn on guard, could hardly keep awake. Back at the camp, meanwhile, everyone had fallen asleep. But Nan awoke suddenly. Something had bumped against her cot, which was placed against one side of her tent. Then she heard stealthy footsteps on the pine needles outside.

Snap had been sleeping in the girls' tent since the boys went to the boat at night. His quick ears caught the sound, and he was out of the tent in a second. Nan heard him snarling and snapping at something. Then he began barking wildly as he chased the intruder off.

Mr. Bobbsey ran out of his tent calling to Snap. Nan and her mother joined him, but Snap did not come back. The barking had stopped suddenly, and there was no sound except the crash of underbrush in the distance.

CHAPTER XII

THE GYPSY

NAN and her father hurried across the clearing, throwing the beams of their flashlights all around. They called Snap continuously, but there was no answering bark nor a glimpse of the shaggy white dog.

"Where *can* he be?" Nan exclaimed.

"He'll be back before long," Mr. Bobbsey assured her. "Snap is probably chasing some animal away up the island. Don't worry about him. He'll come home when he gets hungry. We better go back and get some sleep."

But Nan was very worried about Snap and it was a long time before she finally dozed off.

In the morning, when the boys and Sam came in from the launch, they found the whole family out whistling and calling for Snap.

"What goes?" asked Bert. "Has Snap been chasing a clue again?"

"Yes, I guess so," Freddie answered unhappily. "He chased it so far that he didn't come back."

"Maybe he's lost, Bert," said Flossie, with tears in her eyes.

"Snap couldn't get lost on the island," Bert assured the worried twins. "It isn't big enough. But if he isn't back soon, we'll look for him right after breakfast."

Nan told Sam and the boys about the camp visitor and how Snap had given chase.

Bert let out a long whistle. "I guess the man in the rowboat went ashore instead of coming to see us."

Sam, who had gone across into the woods to call Snap, now came running back to the camp.

"Somebody's busted up the maze again!" he burst out. "I didn't go all the way in, but the bushes near the entrance are broken down!"

"Oh! Our work ruined again!" Bert exclaimed in disgust, and Charlie groaned.

Sam chuckled. "I have to laugh when I think of that fellow tryin' to get away from Snap in the maze," he said. "I don't wonder he busted the hedges down."

The others laughed at this thought too, and Bert said, "Good old Snap. He must have chased the guy in there! No one would go into the labyrinth of his own accord if he was trying to get away fast."

"Maybe the man caught Snap," said Flossie excitedly.

Freddie looked at his father, then asked in a worried voice, "Do you think that Snap could have been dog-naped, Daddy?"

"I hope not," Mr. Bobbsey answered. "There's no worse person than a kidnaper or a dog-naper."

Directly after breakfast the dog hunt started. First the searchers stopped at the maze to see what harm had been done. Several of the bushes which had been transplanted had been knocked down by someone making a hasty retreat through the west side of the labyrinth.

"We can replant these," Charlie said. "They're not damaged much."

The east side was badly trampled. "It looks as though there'd been a battle in here," Bert remarked. "I hope nothing happened to Snap in the fight. Let's get going!"

Mr. Bobbsey suggested that they separate. Sam and the two boys would search through the woods, while Mr. Bobbsey and the younger twins would cruise along the shore in the launch.

Nan decided to remain at the labyrinth to figure out how much new shrubbery would be needed to replace the hedges. Some time later, as she bent to examine one of the broken bushes, Nan heard a muffled sound. It stopped suddenly.

She waited, listening, but the noise did not come again.

"That could have been a dog barking! Snap!" she thought excitedly. Nan tried to figure out where the sound had come from, but it had been too faint and far away for her to tell.

The boys and Sam returned after an unsuccessful search.

"We may as well get to work on the maze," Bert said. "At least Charlie and Nan and I. Sam, I know you want to go fishing with Dad as soon as he comes back. We three can fix the maze ourselves today."

Sam smiled. "I'll catch you some nice big bass for your dinner," he said. "And when Snap comes back, I'll give him a big supper. He's mighty fond o' bass." Sam hurried away toward camp.

Charlie went with him to get a spade. When he returned, the boys joined Nan in setting up the trampled bushes. Then they went just beyond the maze to dig up the new bushes they would need.

At that moment Flossie and Freddie came running toward the older children. "We didn't see Snap anywhere," Freddie reported. "And we went 'way up the shore to where Tommy's house is. Oh dear! I wish Snap would come back!"

"In the meantime you can help us work," Nan

told the younger twins. "Suppose you get the baskets and gather up all the broken branches in the paths."

"Okay," Freddie agreed. He started over to get the baskets, which were stacked beside a tree. Just then he saw a stirring in the thicket at the edge of the woods, near where the older children were working.

"I guess Tommy's coming," Freddie thought. "Maybe he'll know where Snap is."

It was not Tommy who stepped out into the open space, however, but a young woman. She was wearing a bright yellow skirt, a red blouse, and a green scarf over her long black hair. Around her neck hung strings of brilliantly colored beads.

"She's a gypsy," Nan murmured to the boys.

The woman walked quickly to the entrance of the labyrinth. "Good morning," she said. "What are you making here, may I ask? I've never seen anything like it on Blueberry Island."

Nan thought she had never seen such bold, beady, brown eyes as the gypsy's. "Do you live on the island?" she asked.

"Not exactly. We gypsies come here to pick berries every summer. I heard your voices and came to see what was going on."

"We're making a trial labyrinth," Bert told her. Then he explained a little about the design of the maze.

"Will you take me to what you call the center?" asked the young woman eagerly. "I'd like to see how you've made the paths."

"Gladly," Bert answered, leading the way. When they reached the oak tree the gypsy sat down on the broad stump. "You have a seat and everything!" she exclaimed. "I think you are very smart children. Well, I must go back now."

Bert motioned for her to go ahead of him as she rose from the stump, but she shook her head. "After you," she said. "I'd rather follow." She raised one hand and began to finger a string of beads. Suddenly she cried out, "Oh, I've broken my beads!"

The bright red beads flew in all directions. As Bert started to pick them up she stopped him, saying, "Oh, don't bother. They're not worth the trouble." She had caught some of them, he noticed, and had them in her hand.

Bert went first along the twisting paths to the entrance of the labyrinth. Nan, Charlie, and the younger twins were seated on the knoll.

"The dark-haired girl is very pretty and interesting looking," the gypsy said to Bert. "I'd like to tell her fortune. I'll read her palm."

"Nan, would you like to have your palm read?" Bert called as they crossed to the knoll and joined the others.

"Oh, yes!" Nan cried, extending her hand to the gypsy, who sat down beside her.

"I see great happiness for you, my dear," the gypsy said

The woman glanced at the little gold bracelet that gleamed on Nan's arm as she took her hand. Then she bent to study the lines which criss-crossed on the palm.

"I see great happiness for you, my dear," she said. "But first, I see a loss. Have you lost something dear to you lately? If not, you will soon."

"Oh, yes, we've lost Snap!" cried Flossie. "Can you tell where he is from Nan's hand?"

"What is Snap?" asked the woman, looking up at the eager faces around her.

"Our dog," Flossie said. "Our darling dog."

"Is he white and sort of shaggy?" asked the gypsy, dropping Nan's hand. "I saw a dog like that tied to a tree in the woods when I came through this morning!"

"That must be Snap!" exclaimed Freddie. His eyes shone with happiness.

"Wait a minute, Freddie," Bert said. "If Snap were in the woods he would have barked when we were calling him this morning."

"Oh, but this was deep in the woods," the gypsy told them as she jumped up. "Come, I'll lead you to the very spot."

"Oh, yes, let's go," Nan exclaimed, and scrambled to her feet.

The gypsy led the way as the little procession entered the woods beyond the clearing. Bert tried to keep up with the others, but his ankle had begun to throb with pain. Though anxious to find Snap, Bert knew he could not walk much farther.

Dejectedly, the boy turned and limped slowly back toward the clearing. As he came out into the open, his eyes went to the labyrinth which he was so eager to finish. His heart gave a leap, and he stopped still. Over the top of the hedge near the entrance, he could see the head of an animal moving.

"It's a huge, brown bear!" Bert thought wildly.

CHAPTER XIII

LOST!

FOR a moment Bert was too startled to move. A bear on Blueberry Island!

"He's probably heading for camp!" Bert thought, regaining his wits. "I must warn Mother! She's alone there!"

Bert realized that the bear would soon reach the entrance. If the boy hurried, he might be past the opening before the bear found it!

With his injured ankle Bert could not run fast. But he did get by the entrance before the bear appeared. Then he ran faster as fierce growls came from behind him.

Mrs. Bobbsey, in the service tent, had heard the running footsteps. "What is it, Bert?" she asked, coming to the open tent flap.

Bert waved her back as he turned to look for the bear. He had thought it was close on his heels, but it was nowhere in sight.

"A bear was chasing me!" he told her. "Please, Mother, keep inside the tent. I'll go get Dad and Sam."

He hurried to the beach and shouted for the men, who were fishing not far from shore. Then he ran back to the service tent where Mrs. Bobbsey now stood with a large stick in her hands.

"Are you sure you saw a bear, Bert?" she asked.

"Yes, Mother, I truly did."

They heard the boat scraping over the beach, and presently the two fishermen came running through the grove.

"What is the matter?" asked Mr. Bobbsey.

Bert explained what had happened. He was beginning to feel rather silly, since there was no bear in sight.

"Where are the other children, Bert?" Mrs. Bobbsey asked worriedly.

Bert told how the gypsy had come, and was leading the others to the place where she said a dog matching Snap's description was tied to a tree deep in the woods.

"I don't like this," Mrs. Bobbsey said, "even if the gypsy is all right. Besides, that bear may find the children. We must go after them at once!"

Bert and the three grownups hurried across the clearing. As they reached the maze, the searchers were astounded to see a man's head slowly rise over the top of a shrub. He had a bald pate and shifty, greenish eyes.

"Hi, there!" called Bert. "Did—"

The bald head disappeared much faster than it had come into sight. Forgetting his injured ankle, Bert raced to the entrance and dashed into the maze, followed by the others. He and Sam took one route, Mr. and Mrs. Bobbsey the other. When they met, neither group had seen the bald-headed man.

"He must have crashed through the hedges and run into the woods," Mrs. Bobbsey said.

They made an entire circuit of the labyrinth once more, ending at the entrance. There were no broken bushes!

"That man must have been hiding in one of the blind alleys we missed," Mr. Bobbsey concluded. "After we passed him, he ran out."

Bert was staring at the path. Suddenly he walked off and followed it back once more to the oak tree. A little cluster of red beads lay by the stump. They matched a trail of beads which he had noticed along the path. Bert put one of the beads into the pocket of his dungarees. When he met the others, he told them about his discovery.

"That gypsy was marking the way for someone!" he said. "That's why she wanted me to take her around the labyrinth."

"And why she wanted to get all you children away from here," said Mrs. Bobbsey.

"But *what* did that man want in the maze?" Bert asked.

"I haven't the faintest idea," his father replied, as they all hurried across the clearing and into the woods to find Nan, Charlie, and the younger twins.

If Freddie and Flossie haven't seen the bear," Mrs. Bobbsey said, "don't say anything about it to them just now."

The younger twins, meanwhile, together with Nan and Charlie, had been hoping eagerly to find Snap. They had followed the gypsy as she led them farther into the forest. The children stumbled over roots and tangled vines as they pushed aside the leafy branches of the underbrush. Flossie and Freddie were growing tired when the woman finally stopped.

"Go in there between those two crooked trees," she said. "Walk straight ahead for a way, and you'll see the dog."

Charlie dashed ahead eagerly, but Nan said, "That won't be necessary. He'll bark if he's in there. Here, Snap! Here, Snap!" she called.

The gypsy seized Nan's arm roughly. "Go on!" she commanded in a harsh voice. "I tell you there's a dog tied up in there." She gave Nan a shove.

"Don't you push my sister!" Freddie exploded. "You're not a nice lady!"

"Get along in there," replied the woman. "And you too." She gave Flossie a little push.

Nan said quietly but firmly, "Don't touch us!"

Then she took the little twins by the hand and turned her back on the gypsy. "Come on, honeys, we'll see if Snap is here," she said.

At this moment Charlie came running back. "How much farther is—Ooh! Where is she?" he exclaimed. He was staring past Nan. She and the twins turned around.

The gypsy had vanished!

"I guess she didn't like it because I said she wasn't a nice lady," Freddie said.

"She was awful cross!" Flossie added. "I'm glad she's gone."

The children circled the area, calling and whistling for Snap. He did not answer, and they found no dog tied to a tree. At last they had to admit that the gypsy had fooled them.

"She's an old meanie," said Flossie, as the children decided to go back to camp.

"Do you know which way camp is?" Nan asked Charlie. "I don't think I do."

"It's over this way. Follow me," Charlie replied, leading the way.

They scrambled along through the thickets in silence. It was hard going, and they had to rest often.

After what seemed like a long time, Nan said, "Charlie, I'm sure we've passed that tree with the long grapevine on it twice before. Aren't we going in a circle?"

Charlie stopped walking and looked around.

"Do you know which way camp is?" Nan asked Charlie

"It sure does look familiar. I'm afraid we're lost!"

"Let's holler loud. Maybe they'll hear us at camp," Freddie suggested. *"Woo hoo!* Hello! Hello!" he shouted. The others took up the cry. Then they kept quiet for a few seconds.

"Listen! I hear something!" Nan cried. "Someone's whistling."

"It's Tommy!" shouted Charlie as the blueberry boy came into sight carrying his bucket.

"Was that you shouting?" he asked. "What's up?"

"Boy! Are we glad to see you!" exclaimed Charlie gratefully. "We can't find our way out of this jungle, Tommy."

"It is hard, if you don't know the woods," Tommy said. "Did you come to pick blueberries?"

"Oh, no, Tommy. Listen to this." Charlie told him the story.

"A gypsy?" Tommy repeated. "There have never been any gypsies on this island since I can remember. That woman was fooling you."

At that moment Nan happened to look at her arm. "Oh!" she wailed. "My bracelet's gone!"

"You lost it?" Charlie asked.

Nan shook her head. "It couldn't have slipped off. The gypsy must have taken it when she grabbed my arm," Nan declared. "That awful woman!"

"It's a shame," said Tommy. "Come on, I'll lead you back to camp," he offered. "Where's Bert?"

As if in answer Bert's voice came through the trees. "Hi, Charlie! Nan! Where are you?"

"Here we are!" cried Nan. She stumbled as fast as she could after Tommy.

In a moment Bert, Mr. and Mrs. Bobbsey and Sam came into view. "I see you didn't find Snap," Bert said disappointedly.

"I'm so sorry," said Mrs. Bobbsey. "But I'm glad you're all safe."

"The bad lady pushed Nan and took her bracelet, and then she ran away and we were lost," Flossie burst out.

After Nan and Charlie had told the rest of the story, Tommy exclaimed, "Oh! I saw a woman with a bright yellow skirt going into the Whiteside cabin when I came past there about an hour ago."

"She must be the gypsy!" cried Nan. "But if there aren't supposed to be any gypsies on the island, who is she?"

"We'll find out," Mr. Bobbsey declared. "We'll go and call on old Mrs. Whiteside right after lunch." They hurried back to camp.

Tommy was invited to stay and have sandwiches with the family. Then Mr. Bobbsey took them all in the *Tall Timber* to the north end of the island. Tommy left them at the dock but he promised to keep a close watch on the Whiteside cabin in the future.

The old shack was as desolate-looking as ever with the windows still boarded up and the porch falling apart. Mr. Bobbsey knocked loudly three times before the cracked, hoarse voice bade them enter.

Mrs. Whiteside was in the same dark corner in her wheelchair. The room was even more untidy than when the Bobbseys had been there before.

The old woman scowled at the callers, and her only greeting was:

"Well, it's about time you brought my money. Where is it?"

Nan stepped forward a little and said politely, "We didn't bring the money, Mrs. Whiteside. We wanted to ask you if your niece is back. We heard that a young—"

"No, she isn't. Besides, that's none of your business," retorted Mrs. Whiteside rudely.

Bert was not daunted by her unpleasant manner. "We're looking for a young woman dressed as a gypsy," he explained. "We heard that she came into this cabin."

The old lady gave a cackle of laughter. Then she said, "Nobody's been here today. Now—what about my money?"

"As soon as you have proof of your ownership,

we'll see that you get it," Mr. Bobbsey replied.

He opened the door, and the visitors filed out. As they stepped onto the porch Bert tripped on a loose board and nearly fell. Something in the crack caught his eye, and he bent excitedly to look.

CHAPTER XIV

TREETOP DETECTIVES

CAUGHT in the crack of the rickety porch was a red bead. Bert picked it out and put it in his dungaree pocket.

As soon as they were on the launch, Bert took the red bead from his pocket. Then he drew forth the one which he had found in the labyrinth. They matched exactly!

The others had been watching him. "Another clue?" Charlie asked curiously.

Bert nodded. "This *proves* that the gypsy was at Mrs. Whiteside's cabin," he said. "And it proves too, that she's connected in some way with the man who was in the maze today."

"Was another man in our labyrinth?" Nan cried out.

"Yes." Bert quickly told about the bald-headed man, but did not mention the bear. "Then I found some red beads in the maze that had been scattered by the gypsy. She must have been marking a trail for that man!"

"For Pete's sake!" Charlie exclaimed. "I want to see this trail of beads."

"I do too," Nan said excitedly.

When the *Tall Timber* dropped anchor in the camp harbor, Mr. Bobbsey took the three older children to shore first. Then, with a warning from him to be very careful, they started off.

On the way Bert told Nan and Charlie about seeing the bear. "That's why we must watch out," he said.

"If you could see the bear's head above the hedges," said Charlie, "he must have been walking on his hind legs. That seems funny to me. I think bears go on all four feet."

"Usually they do," said Nan, who knew a lot about bears, as did the other twins. "But of course, bears can stand upright."

"It's a prize mystery how he got into the place," said Bert. "And a triple extra one how he disappeared."

"Maybe," Nan guessed, "he's a trick bear, and belongs to the man who lost his toupee. Perhaps he was looking for the toupee and brought the bear along to frighten us."

As she said this, the bushes at the edge of the woods rustled noisily, and Tommy Turner hurried through. "I've got news!" he shouted excitedly. "Come quick!"

The three ran to meet him. "What's up, Tommy?" asked Bert.

"I saw my berry bucket! It was on the porch of the Whitesides' shack as I came past there just now. I didn't dare get it, because an ugly-looking, red-haired man was sitting on the steps."

"Are you sure it's your bucket?" Charlie inquired.

"Oh, yes. There was a streak of red paint on one side."

"Then Pen Whiteside or some friend of his must have taken your berries," Nan declared.

The children were excited. Aunt Emma, the gypsy, and the red-haired man appeared to be friends. Two of the trio were thieves. Was Aunt Emma also dishonest? What was the explanation of the strange things these people had done?

That night Bert and his father decided to sleep on the *Tall Timber* and guard it. Charlie stayed in camp while Sam kept an eye on the maze. There was no disturbance anywhere during the night.

"Nobody came," Flossie said with a sigh, the next morning. "Not even Snap." A tear trickled down her cheek.

"Don't you cry, honey," Bert said. "Do you know what I'm going to do? I'm going to climb to the top of the oak tree and look over the whole island for Snap. I'll take the binoculars up with me."

"I'm with you on that," Charlie said eagerly.

Nan carried the glasses in their leather case. After the three children had run through the maze to the tree, the boys started up the trunk. Bert dangled a thin rope to which Nan would tie the binoculars to be hauled up by him.

"Ready," he called down presently.

Nan tied the rope snugly about the case. "Pull!" she said.

The binoculars rose into the branches slowly and disappeared. A few minutes later Bert called down:

"I can see all around the island." Presently he reported, "There's not a sign of Snap. But I see Whitesides' place. Say, a boat is tied up at their dock!"

"I'm coming up," Nan said.

She climbed onto the broad stump by the oak tree and gave a little jump to reach the lowest branch. As she caught it Nan had a feeling that the stump had moved under her feet but decided that it was just her imagination. She forgot about it entirely as she reached the high branches and Bert handed her the glasses.

Through a gap in the leaves she could get a clear view of the north end of Blueberry Island. As she leveled the binoculars on the Whiteside cabin, Nan saw a young woman come out. She wore a large hat, so Nan could not see her face. The woman went quickly to the boat, where a

"Pull!" Nan said

man in a light raincoat and pulled-down hat was waiting.

"I wonder who they are," Nan remarked. "Anyway, I'm sure the boat is the one with the outboard motor that we saw in Lakeport." She handed the glasses to Charlie.

"But why should it be at the Whiteside dock?" Charlie asked. "Oh, there it goes!" he exclaimed. "Boy, that man really speeds! He's heading straight for Lakeport."

At this moment Flossie and Freddie arrived near the big tree. They were playing hide and seek. As Flossie said, "I see you, Freddie, back of that sticky bush," Tommy Turner hurried up to them.

"Hi!" he said. "Where's Bert?"

"He's up in the oak tree," Flossie told him, pointing to the oak. "Charlie and Nan are 'way up there too."

Tommy hurried over to call to the three. "I have something to tell you."

"We'll be right down," Bert told him.

Nan and Charlie climbed down first, and Bert lowered the glasses. Then he followed.

"Last night," Tommy began his story, "that boat with the outboard motor came by as usual on its way to the boathouse by the Whiteside cabin."

"What!" exclaimed Bert. "Is that boat kept at the Whiteside place?"

"Oh, yes. I see it go past 'most every morning, and it usually comes back in the evening—sometimes not till late at night."

"Go on, Tommy," Nan urged.

"Well, as I said, I saw the motorboat come by just when I went to bed. A little while later something woke me up. I looked out, and there in the moonlight near shore was a rowboat. I couldn't see the face of the man in it, but he had on a light raincoat just like the one the man in the motorboat wears."

"Was he alone in the boat?" asked Charlie.

"Yes," Tommy replied, "but he must have had a heavy load because the rowboat was awful low in the water, and he wasn't going very fast. He was trying to be quiet too, sort of sneaky-like, so I thought."

"I wonder where he was going," Bert said.

Freddie and Flossie suddenly saw Sam coming and ran to meet him. Bert took the opportunity to whisper to Tommy about having seen a bear.

"A bear!" Tommy exclaimed. "There just *aren't* any bears on this island!"

"But I saw it," Bert insisted.

Tommy looked puzzled. "I don't know how to figure what's going on," he said, "but it sure looks as though someone was trying to scare you Bobbseys away from Blueberry Island."

"I'm going to ask Dad to take us back to the

Whitesides' again today," Bert declared. "I want to find out more about those people if I can."

Sam overheard this remark, as he joined the children. "Your dad and mother have gone fishing," he told Bert. "But I guess I can go over there with you, if we're not gone too long."

"We can take the path through the woods opposite the entrance to the maze," Tommy said. "It goes right to the Whiteside place." He led the way.

They walked quickly along the firm, pine-needled path straight through the woods to the tree-lined shore where the Whiteside cabin and boathouse stood.

Bert and Charlie ran to peer inside the tumble-down boathouse. "There's no boat here now," Bert announced as they rejoined Sam. "But I saw oil on the water, so a motorboat must have been moored inside recently."

The callers went to the shack, and Sam knocked on the door several times. There was no answer. He tried the door gently, but it was locked.

"Well, that's that," Bert said glumly. "We have no right to break the door down."

"I'm sure Mrs. Whiteside must be here," Nan said slowly. "I think we *ought* to look inside. She may be ill and need help. Can't you get the door open, Sam?"

Sam took a knife from his pocket. "This might turn the lock," he said. He inserted an odd-looking blade of his knife into the lock. It turned, and he opened the rickety door, which swung inward on loudly squeaking hinges.

Bert entered the cabin first, with the others close behind him. In the dark interior they could see the empty wheelchair in a corner and the usual disorder of clothing around the room.

"Mrs. Whiteside, are you here?" Nan called out. "If you need—"

At that moment Flossie gave a frightened shriek.

CHAPTER XV

AN ODD CAVE

WHEN Flossie screamed, everyone turned to look at her. In the dim light they could see what had frightened the little girl. It was the head of a bear!

"It's not real. It's a fake," said Nan quickly.

"Hot diggity! I'll bet that's what I saw!" Bert exclaimed as he took the brown, shaggy head from a low chest by the door. "No wonder it fooled me." Then he told Flossie and Freddie about seeing the "bear" in the maze.

"There's the rest of him," Charlie said, grinning, and pointing to a furry heap on a chair.

"That's the only kind of bear that could be on Blueberry Island," Tommy said, laughing. "A make-believe one."

"Pen Whiteside, or somebody else who lives here, must like to dress up," observed Nan. "Here's a box of wigs and toupees of all colors. There's a red mustache, too."

"Oh, that's what the man in the boathouse had," Freddie cried excitedly. "Didn't he, Flossie?"

"Yes, and Snap found a toupee in the maze," his twin added. "Mr. Pen Whiteside must have lots of different kinds of hair."

"He's really bald," said Bert. "That is, if he's the one we saw in the maze yesterday."

"Yes," Sam spoke up. "He didn't wear a wig then because he probably had the bear head over his bald top."

Bert said to Charlie, "That man who came to the *Tall Timber* during the night had red hair, and a mustache." Charlie nodded.

Flossie had been staring around the room and now ventured to take a few steps forward. "I see Mrs. Whiteside's dress and her shawl," she remarked. "They're on her wheelchair."

"And I think," said Charlie, "that probably she wears this gray wig." He took one from a box.

"Maybe Mrs. Whiteside is in the other room," Freddie suggested, looking at the closed door.

"We'll soon find out," Bert declared and knocked on the door. When there was no answer, he opened it wide.

They could see that the room beyond was a small bedroom. In it were a bed and a cracked mirror over a table. The rest of the space was filled with boxes and suitcases, from which articles of clothing trailed over the floor. Other wearing apparel was hung on nails driven into the bare walls. Nan and Flossie darted over to them.

"Here's the gypsy's skirt!" Nan cried, holding up the gay, yellow garment.

"Oh, I see the blue lady's dress!" Flossie shouted, and pointed to a bright blue gown hanging with the others against the wall.

"Here's a yellow wig," Charlie said, lifting the half-opened cover of a box near by. It was a blond, curly hairpiece. "And here is a collection of rubber noses and ears. Look!" He slipped a hooked nose over his own straight one.

"That's the blue lady's nose!" Flossie cried, "and *she* had yellow hair—I mean the lady I saw take money from Mrs. Rudd's purse."

The Bobbsey twins looked at one another, then at Charlie and Sam. *They had solved the mystery of the Lakeport thieves!*

"We must tell the police at once!" Nan said. "Come on."

"I wonder where the thieves hid what they stole," Bert said, gazing about.

"We'd better not look," Sam advised. "Let's leave that to the police. After all, we have no business snooping around like this even though the people are thieves."

"The bad man hid some of the things on our boat," Flossie declared.

"That probably was part of the loot," Charlie agreed, "and the diamond ring Nan found, too."

"I don't think the five hundred dollars ever belonged to that mean old Mrs. Whiteside," Freddie said, and the others nodded.

"I wonder if we'll ever find the real owner," Nan said.

During this conversation, Tommy had been looking for his berry bucket. He came dashing out of a lean-to at the rear. "I found my bucket," he exclaimed. "Would it be all right to take it now, Sam?"

"I'd leave it here if I were you, Tommy," Bert spoke up. "The Whitesides would know you'd been here, and they might skip out before the police came. What else did you see in there?"

"Nothing except some funny-looking brown cloth bags heaped up in a corner, and a couple of battered pans, and a gasoline stove."

Bert looked startled. "How big were the bags?" he asked.

"Oh, about like this," Tommy held out his arms. "I'd say they were like small flour sacks."

"Wow!" Bert could not help exploding. "Just like the one we found on the *Tall Timber!*"

All the way back through the woods, Nan was silent. But when they reached the entrance to the maze, she stopped.

"I s'pose you'll think I'm silly," she told the others. "But when I jumped off the big stump to climb the oak tree, I had the funniest feeling that the stump—moved. Let's go and take another look at it."

She ran down the main path, leading the way to the oak tree. The others trailed her quickly. When they reached the stump, it looked the same as ever—broad and solid, and surrounded by low-growing, scrubby weeds.

"Well, there's one way to find out," said Bert. "We'll give it a good push."

"I'll do it, Bert," said Sam. He leaned down and braced himself and gave the stump a mighty heave.

To everyone's amazement, the stump was so light that Sam lost his balance and fell over with the stump in his arms!

"It's hollow!" cried Charlie.

"Oh, look!" screamed Flossie. She was pointing to a narrow excavation which the stump had covered.

"Steps!" gasped Freddie. "Going down into the ground!"

Sam scrambled to his feet while they all stared at the dugout. It was about three feet across and had been well covered by the huge stump. Wooden boards lined the cavity, and a flight of crude steps of rotting wood led down some six feet below.

"This is how the man and the 'bear' disappeared," Bert said. "It's a secret passage!"

Sam had been examining the overturned stump, an amazed expression on his jolly face. "For land's sake," he muttered. "What's going on around here anyway? There's a cleat nailed inside this, so's the stump could be pulled back over the hole after the man went down inside."

Freddie ran to look at it. "Bert," he cried, "that's like the sharp thing on the log out there by the edge of the woods where I tore my pants."

"That must have been the first cover for this dugout," Bert said. "It was rotted, so the thieves made a new one out of the stump."

"What's down there?" asked Freddie, bending over the cavity.

"I'll go and see," Bert replied, starting down the steps. "If everything's all right, I'll call back."

"I don't feel right letting you go down in that hole alone, Bert," protested Sam uneasily. "I'm goin' with you."

He followed the boy, while the others waited breathlessly. In a few moments Bert called to Charlie and the twins to come down. They found themselves in a large cave which extended for several feet under the labyrinth and beyond.

"Jingo!" Tommy exclaimed in a low voice. "I never dreamed that there was such a place on the island!"

"Look over there," Nan said. "Isn't that a little pond?" She pointed across the dark space to where a slight glimmer shone dimly.

"Yes," Bert agreed. "That must be an inlet from the lake that comes inside the cave and forms this pond. The bushes on the bank must hide the opening from the lake."

"I see a boat tied just inside the bushes," Charlie said, staring. "It's a small, empty rowboat."

"I see it!" Flossie exclaimed excitedly.

"That's the boat I 'most fell into when I leaned over the bushes too far."

"Flossie's right," Charlie said. "This is just about where the knoll is."

"No wonder the boat disappeared so fast," Bert remarked.

"I'll bet—" Tommy began, but stopped short. There was a sudden, harsh sound like the rattling of chains. It came from the darkest corner of the cave.

CHAPTER XVI

HIDDEN TREASURES

AS THE strange rattling and scraping noise continued in the corner of the cave, Sam muttered, "We'd better get out of here fast!"

He tried to take Freddie's hand, but the little boy held back as he stared into the darkness. "Why, it's Snap!" Freddie screamed excitedly.

"You're right!" cried Bert, darting across the damp, uneven floor of the cave.

Nan followed her twin. "Oh, the poor darling! Why doesn't he bark?"

Charlie and Tommy rushed toward the corner too. Now the chains were clanking more rapidly as a white blur whirled and bounced like a small cyclone.

Flossie had let go of Sam's hand to run with Freddie and the others to where the white dog was trying to break loose from the chain that held him.

Bert knelt to undo the heavy collar around Snap's neck. "Good old boy! We'll get you out of here fast."

"Poor Snap's nose is all bound up," said Nan. "That's why he couldn't bark to tell us he was here!" She quickly removed the strap that was wound about Snap's muzzle.

Flossie and Freddie put their arms around the dog's neck as soon as he was free. He could not restrain his happiness and cavorted about, whining with joy and uttering short, sharp barks.

"I thought I heard Snap yesterday in the labyrinth," Nan declared. "His barking was muffled. Then it stopped. I guess that's when somebody put the strap around his nose."

Snap ran to the foot of the steps and then back to his beloved playmates, whining anxiously.

"He wants you to get out of this hole," Sam said. "And so do I."

"All right, Sam, we'll come now. We've found Snap, and we know how those people in our maze disappeared," Bert answered.

"And we found where the man in the rowboat hid," Flossie added. "Now you know I saw him."

"We certainly do, honey," Nan said.

Nan was last in line when they started up the crude stairway. As her foot touched the first step Nan noticed a dark heap against the wall on the under side of the open steps. She decided to investigate and stepped around to the back.

"Oh, look!" she called in a hushed voice.

Bert, Charlie, and Tommy were back at her side in a second, as she bent over a pile of brown cloth bags. Each was bulging.

"Wowee!" Bert exclaimed softly, as he lifted one. "This is heavy!"

"Those are like the empty bags I saw in the

Whiteside cabin," Tommy said excitedly. "What's in them?"

Bert unfastened the stout cord which bound the top of one. He shook the bag a little, and several coins rolled out. Then a shining gold bracelet followed.

"My lost bracelet!" Nan gasped. She caught it and slid it on her arm. "This loot is probably the gypsy's."

"There must be two thieves," Bert said thoughtfully, "and probably they're the two we saw in the boat with the outboard motor."

"I'm glad they're away today," Flossie said. "But why did they steal Snap and tie him up?"

"That's easy," said Charlie. "Snap was too wise about this place. They were afraid he would show us the stump's secret."

As though he had heard his name, the white dog came to the top of the steps and barked.

"Snap wants you to come up here," Sam called from above. "What's keeping you?"

"We're coming now," Nan called back.

"Yes, we'd better scram," Tommy said. "Bert, hurry and tie up that bag."

Bert fastened the cord securely. Then he and the two boys followed Nan up the steps. Sam replaced the stump over the dugout.

"We found more loot!" Charlie announced excitedly, as Nan showed her recovered bracelet.

"Well, that sure beats everything," Sam said.

As they hurried across the clearing, Tommy said, "I'll bet Pen Whiteside and his mother brought the stuff they stole to their boathouse in the motorboat. Then Pen took it to the cave at night in the rowboat."

"But the rowboat was tied here," Charlie said.

"Sure," said Bert. "He came on foot to get it —used that trail from his cabin to the maze."

Out in the launch Mr. and Mrs. Bobbsey heard Snap barking and came ashore at once. They hurried up the beach to meet Sam and the children.

"Oh, Mommy, Daddy!" screamed Flossie. "The stump isn't a stump at all, and Snap was chained up under it!"

"We found a pond under the ground and a boat there too," Freddie added excitedly.

It took nearly ten minutes to tell the whole story. The twins' parents shook their heads in amazement. Then Mr. Bobbsey said, "We must report this to the police at once. There's no time to waste."

"I'd better stay here and guard our camp," Sam said.

Mrs. Bobbsey decided to remain on the island also. "If anyone bothers us," she said with a chuckle, "Sam and I will hide in the maze! But seriously, I doubt that those thieves will come here. As soon as they realize we've found Snap, they'll run away as fast as they can to avoid the police."

"We'd better get going," Bert urged. "It would be a shame if they should escape."

"Right you are, Bert," his father said. Soon he and the children were aboard the *Tall Timber,* heading for Lakeport.

"Golly!" exclaimed Tommy. "This is more excitement than I've had in my whole life!"

"That's because you haven't known the twins before this summer," Charlie told him, chuckling.

"I'm sure glad I do know them," Tommy replied. "They've brought me good luck with the blueberries, too. I made more money this summer than ever before."

"That's fine, Tommy," said Nan and Bert together.

The conversation turned to the mystery. "It looks," said Nan, "as though the gypsy, old Mrs. Whiteside, and the blue lady with the big nose and the yellow hair might be all the same person."

"You mean," said Flossie, "that she isn't really lame and doesn't have to stay in a wheelchair?"

"Yes, and she's clever at disguises," Nan answered. "Certainly the gypsy and Mrs. Whiteside didn't look alike."

"No, they didn't," Freddie agreed. "And they

didn't talk alike. That lady's a good actress."

"It's my guess," Bert put in, "that her name isn't Whiteside."

"Maybe the police will recognize her," Charlie remarked.

Presently Mr. Bobbsey said he thought this was one of the most exciting vacations the Bobbseys had ever had. "We'll have to break camp tomorrow," he told them as he guided the boat toward the dock in the Bobbsey lumberyard. "I, for one, will be sorry to do it."

"So will I," chorused the twins and Charlie.

Tommy sighed. "I'll miss you all. Blueberry Island won't be the same without the Bobbseys and Charlie!"

"You must come back to supper with us tonight, Tommy," Nan said. "We'll have a bonfire to celebrate our last night in camp."

Just as the launch drew near the lumberyard dock, a boat with a powerful outboard motor suddenly shot into the lake and headed directly toward them. It carried two people; a woman holding a big hat, and a man in a light raincoat, his brimmed hat pulled low.

"Look!" Bert exclaimed. "Here come the very people we want to capture!"

CHAPTER XVII

AN EXCITING CHASE

FOR a moment it looked as though the speeding boat would run squarely into the *Tall Timber.* Mr. Bobbsey swerved quickly to avoid a collision.

"Whew!" exclaimed Bert, as the thieves' boat turned and roared up the lake. "Dad, aren't you going to chase it?"

"No. The police must do that," his father said firmly and took his own craft into the boathouse.

"Maybe the police are on their trail already," Nan suggested, "and that's why they're going so fast."

"It did look as if they were making a swift getaway from someone," her father agreed, as everyone clambered out of the launch. "But Bert, suppose you go phone the police anyway, and tell them everything you found out on the island."

As Bert dashed to the lumberyard office, Freddie cried, "Listen! I hear a police car!" There was the sound of a siren from the next block.

"They *are* chasing someone," Nan said excitedly. "If the police come this way, let's tell them about the people in the motorboat." But unfortunately the officers' car did not turn in their direction.

Presently Bert returned out of breath. "Chief Malone says we ought to get ten medals! The police launch is coming past here, and we're to follow it to that good dock on the north end where we landed once."

"Why aren't the policemen going right to the Whitesides'?" Freddie asked.

"I suppose," his father replied, "Chief Malone doesn't want the Whitesides to know the police are coming."

"You mean they might run away in their own boat?"

"That's right, Freddie," Mr. Bobbsey answered. "We'll run up the other side of Blueberry Island and tramp across to the shack." He pulled out into the lake once more and waited for the police. In a few minutes they spotted the launch with Chief Malone and five other officers aboard. The *Tall Timber* took off after it.

"Wow! Look at 'em go!" Charlie exclaimed.

The twins' father put on full speed too, and

the launches fairly flew across the water.

"I hope we can reach the cabin before the Whitesides get away," said Bert.

"They're making swell time," Tommy said as he watched the trail of foam from the police boat.

"So are we," Bert said tensely as his father swung the wheel so the *Tall Timber* would follow the west shore of the Blueberry Island toward the north end.

Moments later, the Bobbsey launch pulled up right behind the police boat, and the children scrambled out to show Chief Malone the way to the Whiteside cabin.

"I've got to tell Mother about this," Tommy said, running toward his house. "I'll see you."

Three of the policemen went ahead with the chief, but the other officer stayed with the driver of the police boat.

"Stay a good distance behind," the chief ordered the children as they started off.

Bert and Charlie followed the officers along the wooded path as closely as the chief allowed. Flossie and Freddie had hard work keeping up with them, so Mr. Bobbsey and Nan waited for the smaller twins. They reached the Whiteside cabin just as the police were breaking down the door, which Sam had managed to lock after the children's earlier visit.

"No one answered the chief's knock," Bert reported. "I guess the Whitesides have gone."

"Or never came here after we saw them," Nan guessed.

"Is their boat gone?" asked Freddie, looking at the rickety boathouse.

"Freddie, that's a thought!" Bert exclaimed, and ran to peer through a wide crack in its wall. "Nothing in here!" he called.

Mr. Bobbsey frowned. "They've escaped. We're too late."

"Maybe they're hiding," Charlie said. "Let's go in the house."

They found the officers searching about in the main room.

"Look!" said the chief to his men, holding up a plain red dress. "This is the kind of dress the clerk in Bard's jewelry store said the shoplifter was wearing when she took a tray full of jewelry."

"You're right, Chief," answered a policeman named Chris. "And over on that chair is the black outfit the so-called old woman wore when she was in Flynn's last Saturday. She stole six pocketbooks that day."

"She knocked me right over," Flossie said, and told what had happened to her.

"Too bad," Chief Malone said, then smiled. "I guess bad people don't have good manners. Well, boys, there's nobody here now. Let's go!"

"There's one other place to look," Bert spoke

up. "Under the floor." He had been standing near one of the half-opened boxes which littered the larger room. "This floor isn't solid! It moved right under my feet! Maybe there's a secret cellar."

Chief Malone and one of the policemen darted over. Together they lifted the board on which Bert had stood.

"Oh!" exclaimed the children.

In the small storage space underneath crouched a woman!

She had short brown hair and wore a tight-fitting blue dress. But there was no question as to her identity. Her beady brown eyes gave her away.

"Mrs. Whiteside!" the boys exclaimed.

"The gypsy!" the girls cried out.

"Not any more," said Chief Malone, as the woman straightened up, glaring at everyone. "This is Mrs. Minnie Jones. Minnie, where is your husband?"

The woman continued to stare at them all but refused to speak.

"Examine the rest of the floor, boys," ordered Chief Malone. "Chris, go outside and search underneath the shack. Pen may have a hiding place too."

As the chief watched Mrs. Jones, he said, "Penman Jones and his wife are wanted in many places for forgery, robbery, and shoplifting."

In the small storage space underneath
crouched a woman!

Mrs. Jones's eyes suddenly lighted on the bracelet which gleamed on Nan's arm. The woman's face turned pale.

Nan saw this and said quickly, "Yes, we found the stolen things in the cave, and our dog you chained up there, this morning."

Officer Chris returned, saying no one was under the shack. At the same moment Tommy Turner came rushing in. "Mother says that just before you got here, the motorboat went south along the shore with the man in it!"

As Tommy paused for breath, Bert said excitedly, "Penman Jones! He's gone to the cave to get the loot! I'll show you the path to it, Chief."

"Fine," the officer agreed. "Chris, take this woman to our launch and bring her with you to the cave." He turned to Nan. "Will you show the men where it is?"

Mr. Bobbsey answered for her. "I'll drive the *Tall Timber,*" he offered, "and the police launch can follow us. Freddie and Flossie, you come with Nan and me."

As everyone hurried from the cabin, the chief said to Bert and Charlie, "Could Penman get his big boat through the opening into the underground pond? Is the opening large enough?"

"Oh, yes," Bert replied. "We figured the reason he didn't go there in it usually was because of the noise of the motor."

"You mean," said the chief, "that if you children had heard the motor, you would have found out about the cave much sooner."

Bert grinned. "That's right." Then he became serious. "If Pen is there, I only hope he doesn't escape before we can block him."

"We'll catch him," Tommy said confidently. "Pen hasn't had time yet to gather up all his loot and get out of the cave."

"Right," Bert agreed. "If the chief and these men don't catch him, the police in the launch will."

The chief and his party sped along the path through the woods. Then Bert led the three officers into the maze and along the twisting paths. The chief looked around and smiled. "You Bobbseys certainly gave the man a hard time with this puzzle contraption," he said. "I can just see baldheaded Jones, alias Whiteside, losing one of his toupees in the shrubbery!"

The chief was still chuckling as Bert and Charlie lifted the stump and disclosed the flight of steps. "Well, this *is* something!" the officer exclaimed.

He and the two policemen led the way, with the boys close behind them. Bert instantly looked behind the steps for the loot.

"It's gone!" he shouted. "The bags have been taken—every one of them!"

The police officers continued to rush forward, and now Bert followed. In a moment he saw the prow of Pen Jones's motorboat pushed into the bushes at the opening from the inlet. Then he saw a crouching man making his way through the cave toward it.

"There he goes!" Bert cried.

There was much shouting and confusion as the officers ran after the man, but Pen jumped into his boat and started the motor. Before the police could reach him, the boat backed out of the cave.

"Too late," said Charlie in disgust.

Bert set his jaw grimly. "If only Dad and the three other cops get here in time!" he thought tensely.

CHAPTER XVIII

A WONDERFUL REWARD

MEANWHILE, Mr. Bobbsey, Nan, and the younger twins had hurried back through the woods to the dock.

The policeman named Chris followed close behind with his prisoner.

Flossie kept looking back at the woman curiously. Finally she asked her, "Are you really a gypsy?"

Mrs. Penman Jones laughed harshly. "Of course not. But I had you all fooled, didn't I? I'm good at make-up."

"I'll say you are," Officer Chris stated. "You had the town in an uproar with your fancy-dress tricks."

Nan asked Mrs. Jones if she had lost a diamond ring in the woods.

"Yes, I did. My engagement ring. You probably think I stole it. Where is the ring?"

"At police headquarters," Nan replied, and the woman shrugged.

Freddie scowled at her and said, "You took Tommy's big, full pail of blueberries and ate 'em all up. He needs the money for them."

Mrs. Jones fairly shouted, "Oh, don't talk to me about blueberries at a time like this!"

When the group reached the dock, Chris said, "Our boat will trail yours, Mr. Bobbsey, to the cave." He then explained to the pilot of the police launch and to the other officer what the plan was.

"We have Mrs. Jones here," he said. "Her husband will soon be a prisoner too, we hope."

He led Mrs. Jones aboard. Then the Bobbseys climbed into the *Tall Timber,* and the two launches started off.

The *Tall Timber* rounded the end of the island and roared toward the southern part, kicking up a trail of waves and foam.

"You're making the policemen rock, Daddy," Flossie observed. Though everyone was tense, this made them all laugh.

Presently Mr. Bobbsey slowed down. "Watch for the entrance to the cave," he said.

Nan nodded. "It's under the knoll—the highest place along the shore."

"It's pretty hard to find," Freddie remarked, as he stared at the shore.

"Yes," said Nan. "The vines and trees and

bushes grow so far down on the banks that they hide the opening."

"There's the knoll!" Flossie finally exclaimed excitedly.

"And there's the underground inlet to the cave. I know it is!" Nan called out. "Shall I signal to the police?" she asked.

"Yes."

To do this, Nan slipped out of the cabin and climbed onto the roof. She waved, pointing toward the shore.

At once the police launch put on power to pass the Bobbseys and investi-

gate. But before it reached the *Tall Timber,* there was a sudden disturbance at the inlet. The green curtain of shrubbery and vines was violently parted. A motorboat shot out of the opening.

Nan shrieked, "Stop!" but the pilot of the boat paid no attention.

"That's Mr. Penman!" exclaimed Flossie.

"Get him!" cried Freddie, jumping up and down inside the cabin.

The police launch bore down on the thief and crowded his boat to the shore. Pen Jones was trapped and forced to stop.

The Bobbseys watched as the two burly officers took the captured man from his boat and put him aboard the police launch with his wife. Then his motorboat was tied to the stern of the launch.

Officer Chris waved to the Bobbseys. "Good work!" he called. "Now we'll pick up the chief and the other fellows, and take Pen's boat and the loot to town. The bags of stolen jewelry and other things are all here."

"Those kids," Mrs. Jones said to her husband, "found out everything."

Penman Jones gave the Bobbsey boat a dark look. "Everything?"

"Everything," Officer Chris said, "except why you hid the clothes and that sack of loot on Mr. Bobbsey's boat."

"I was running away after a robbery and nearly got caught," Pen answered. "Their boathouse was open, and it would have made a good place for me to change disguises. But those two—" he pointed over to Freddie and Flossie, "came along, and I had to hide the things in a hurry. So I hid them in the boat."

Meanwhile, on the *Tall Timber,* Nan asked her father to draw nearer the police launch. "I'd like to ask those Joneses a few questions," she said.

When the two boats were closer, she called over to Pen:

"Did you ruin the cord paths we had laid out, and put a cord across the entrance?"

"Yes," he admitted sullenly.

"And later, did you knock down part of the hedge?" Nan asked.

"Yes," said Pen. "Your dog gave me a bad time until my wife came along and helped me capture him."

"Good old Snap!" said Nan.

"You're not lame, and you lost a green tie?" Freddie asked Pen. "And Mrs. Jones didn't lose the five hundred dollars Snap found?"

"That's right. You kids guessed all the answers. You're too smart!"

At that moment Flossie caught sight of Mrs. Bobbsey on the shore above. "There's Mother!" she shouted joyfully.

"And Sam, and Bert and Charlie, and the policemen!" added Freddie in high excitement, as the group appeared one by one on the edge of the knoll.

The boats drew as close to shore as they dared. Quickly Chris and the chief exchanged stories. Chief Malone said that as soon as his party had seen Penman Jones escaping in his boat, they had rushed up out of the cave and over to the knoll.

"I'm glad you got here in time," he told Chris. "We'll meet you at the camp dock. But before you go, I want to tell the Bobbsey twins and their friends something."

He congratulated them on the success of the search. "The police and the people of Lakeport give you their thanks and gratitude!" he said. "You've caught two very clever people, and you've found many things stolen from Lakeport citizens."

The campers smiled, and Nan said, "We're glad we could help. It was fun."

"And exciting," Bert added. "Being detectives made a swell camping trip."

The chief chuckled, then the three boats set off for the camp dock. The *Tall Timber* reached the small harbor first and waited while Sam rowed the chief and his two men across the clear green water. They climbed aboard and called good-by.

The police launch, with Pen's motorboat trailing, hurried away with the prisoners and recovered valuables. Sam rowed Mr. Bobbsey, Nan, and the younger twins ashore. Mrs. Bobbsey, Tommy, Bert, Charlie, and Sam met them on the beach. Snap was there too, wagging his tail excitedly.

"Sam has a bonfire laid for tonight's celebration, Tommy," Mrs. Bobbsey said. "Would you like to spend the night with the boys? We have an extra sleeping bag."

"That would be neat!" Tommy exclaimed. "I'll ask Mother right away. She'll want to hear about the Joneses, too." He disappeared on a run across the clearing and into the woods. He returned half an hour later. "I can stay," he said.

The bonfire celebration was a great success that evening, but Bert noticed that Tommy had become quiet.

"Is anything wrong, Tom?" he asked in a low voice.

The other boy nodded. "The man who owns our end of the island is going to tear down all the cabins. We won't be able to stay here."

"What a shame!" Bert exclaimed. "You've done so well with your berry picking."

"Yes, I'll miss it."

Mr. Bobbsey had overheard the conversation. "I may be able to help you, Tommy, so don't worry. I'm sure you can stay on Blueberry Island. Have a good time tonight."

Tommy's face lit up with a relieved smile, and he did have a good time the rest of the evening. "I wouldn't have missed this past week for anything!" he exclaimed, as he crawled into his sleeping bag next to Bert and Charlie.

The next morning when they were bidding one another good-by Charlie said, "Remember, Tommy, you're coming to stay with me when the school fair is on."

"I won't forget," the boy answered happily. He went to stand on the high knoll and waved to the Bobbseys and Charlie and Sam as the *Tall Timber* headed across the water for Lakeport.

As it nosed into the boathouse at the lumberyard, Flossie sighed. "I guess all our 'citements are over." Then she added brightly, "Anyway, I'm glad we're home so we can see Dinah and Snoop again and tell them about everything."

On the way home in the station wagon, Sam stopped to let Charlie out at his house.

"It was great, just great," said Charlie as he stepped out and picked up his duffle bag. "Thank you, Mr. and Mrs. Bobbsey, for everything. Bert, I'll be seeing you. 'By, everybody."

"We couldn't have solved the mystery without you," Bert called.

As the Bobbseys drove up to their own house, Dinah was watching for them and opened the front door. "I'm sure glad to see you all," she said, smiling. Then she added, "You got a big fat letter Friday. It says on the envelope, 'Bobbsey Twins!' "

Bert ran in to take the letter from the living room mantelpiece. He tore open the envelope.

"Say!" he exclaimed. "Nan, Freddie, Flossie, this is from a Mrs. Emma Ballard in Hightown. She says she lost the money we found!"

The children clustered excitedly around Bert, and Mr. and Mrs. Bobbsey came to listen too, as Bert began to read:

" 'Dear Bobbsey Twins:

" 'I am so happy and relieved that you found my money. It was foolish of me to lose it, but I am very old and sometimes I do things that don't turn out just right. But I need the five hundred dollars badly. Actually, it is only four hundred and ninety dollars. I spent ten of what I received from my niece.

"The foolish part was that I asked her to give it to me in cash. We met at the railroad station, on Friday, June 24th. After she handed me the money in a stack with a purple band around it, she took a train. I had an hour to wait for mine.

" 'I realized that all this time a man had been watching us, and I got worried because of all the purses that had been snatched in Lakeport. So I thought I'd fool him.

" 'I went across the street to a store and bought a game of toy money. Then, in the ladies' lounge, I put the four hundred and ninety dollars in with the play money. The ten dollars and my railroad ticket and other things I hid in my coat pocket.

" 'After that I bought several things at other stores and had a lot of bundles to carry. I started out of the store for a walk by the lake before train time, when some woman snatched my purse and ran off. But I didn't care because it was old, and there wasn't anything in it!

" 'But alas, when I got home, my precious game with the real money in it was gone. Where did you find it? The only thing I can think of is that I dropped the package as I was walking along the lake.

" 'A shaggy white dog came running up to me, and I played with him. Maybe I dropped the package then. I didn't notice, because I had to hurry to the train. Perhaps the dog picked up the bag and ran off with it.' "

"Snap!" exclaimed Flossie. "Oh you nice, naughty, funny dog!"

"He's all of that," Bert agreed. "Dad, do you think Aunt Emma Ballard is really the one who lost the money?"

"It certainly sounds so."

"Oh here's something else," Bert said, as he turned the page. He read:

" 'P.S. If you want to check my story, call my niece's bank, the First National, in Westover, where she lives. Her name, too, is Emma Ballard.' "

"Oh, do phone there the first thing in the morning," Freddie begged.

Mr. Bobbsey did just that on Monday morning, and came away from the telephone smiling. The cashier had said the story was true. He himself had seen the twins' notice in the Lakeport paper and had given it to the younger Emma Ballard. She in turn had told her aunt about it.

"Let's phone Chief Malone right away and tell him, so he can send the money to Aunt Emma," Nan exclaimed.

Once more Mr. Bobbsey went to the phone. After the call he said, "The police will get in touch at once with Mrs. Ballard."

That evening when he came home from his office, Mr. Bobbsey wore a broad grin. "This is our day for good fortune," he said.

"You mean something else nice happened?" Freddie asked.

His father nodded. "I got in touch with Mr. Harper this morning about the property on Blueberry Island. He is going to keep it after all. This fall he is going to rebuild his cabins and will have them ready next summer. I told him about the Turners, and he says he'll be glad to rent one to them for the same price they paid this year."

"Oh Dad, that's neat!" exclaimed Bert. "I'll phone Charlie about it. And we must go over to Blueberry Island and tell Tommy as soon as we can."

"Yes," his father agreed. "And here's another bit of news. Mr. Harper knew about the cave but thought it had been sealed off years ago. That's why he didn't tell us about it."

Two days went by before Mr. Bobbsey could take the children to Blueberry Island. In the meantime another letter came addressed to the twins. It read:

"The Citizens League of Lakeport wishes to express its gratitude to the Bobbsey twins for their aid in ridding the city of an undesirable element which was causing distress to its citizens and merchants. We enclose a check for the five hundred dollars reward which was offered for this service."

"Wow!" cried Bert and Nan in unison.

"Oh! For us?" asked Freddie in a bewildered tone.

"Some of it belongs to Snap and Charlie and Tommy and Sam and Mother and Daddy," Flossie declared.

For an hour the twins talked in excited whispers about a plan Nan suggested for using a good portion of the money. Their parents approved.

The next day the Bobbseys made the trip to Blueberry Island, and Charlie went along, too. They found Tommy and his mother outside their cabin with the two smaller children.

The thin little woman smiled warmly. "Tommy has talked constantly about the twins and Charlie ever since you left," she said. "I'm so glad you came back to see us."

"We've brought a picnic lunch, Mrs. Turner," the twins' mother said, "and we want you and the children to share it with us while we tell you some news."

While Nan helped her unpack the hard-boiled eggs, sandwiches, and fruit, Mrs. Bobbsey told Mrs. Turner and Tommy how Mr. Harper had decided not to sell his property but instead to remodel the cabins; and how he had promised to let the Turners have one of them without having to pay more rent for it.

"Oh, how wonderful!" exclaimed Tommy and his mother together. Then Tommy grinned. "And nothing extra for the cave?"

"No, nor the labyrinth either," Bert said, grinning back.

"You'll all have to come over and we'll play cops and robbers," Tommy insisted.

Mrs. Bobbsey laughed. "Isn't that what you were doing here for a whole week?" she asked. "And now, Bert, suppose you tell Tommy your other news."

"We twins," Bert said, "were given the five hundred dollars reward for finding Penman Jones and his wife. Of course, some of it belongs to you, Tommy, and to Charlie and Sam. But Charlie and Nan and Freddie and Flossie and I want to use our share to set you up in the business of growing big, cultivated blueberries. Mr. Harper says you may plant them here on his property where they grow so well, and you won't have to roam all through the woods to get them. You can work up a neat trade in Lakeport."

"And every summer will be a big one for the berry business," added Charlie. "We'll be your best customers."

Tommy was speechless for a moment. Then he gasped, "Why—why, this is too swell to be true!"

"It's marvelous," said Mrs. Turner, and there were tears in her eyes. "The Bobbsey twins and Charlie Mason are just the nicest people in the whole world!"

"And Dinah's the best cook in the whole world," said Freddie. "I wish we had one of her pies in our lunch."

Tommy's eyes sparkled. "Would a Turner blueberry pie do?" he asked. "Mother just took one out of the oven."

THE BOBBSEY TWINS®

CLASSIC EDITIONS

1 THE BOBBSEY TWINS OF LAKEPORT
2 THE BOBBSEY TWINS' ADVENTURE IN THE COUNTRY
3 THE BOBBSEY TWINS: THE SECRET AT THE SEASHORE
4 THE BOBBSEY TWINS' MYSTERY AT SCHOOL
5 THE BOBBSEY TWINS AND THE MYSTERY AT SNOW LODGE
6 THE BOBBSEY TWINS ON A HOUSEBOAT
7 THE BOBBSEY TWINS' MYSTERY AT MEADOWBROOK
8 THE BOBBSEY TWINS' BIG ADVENTURE AT HOME
9 THE BOBBSEY TWINS' SEARCH IN THE GREAT CITY
10 THE BOBBSEY TWINS ON BLUEBERRY ISLAND
11 THE BOBBSEY TWINS' MYSTERY ON THE DEEP BLUE SEA
12 THE BOBBSEY TWINS' ADVENTURE IN WASHINGTON